Y0-EKR-967

RED ASSCHER
Living in Fear

P. C. CHINICK

A Russian Hill Press Book
United States • United Kingdom • Australia

Russian Hill Press

The publisher bears no responsibility for the quality of
information provided through author or third party websites and
does not have any control over, nor assumes any responsibility
for information contained in these sites.

Copyright 2014 by P. C. Chinick

All rights reserved, including the right to reproduce this book or
portions thereof in any form whatsoever.

Red Asscher is a work of historical fiction. Apart from the well-
known actual people, events and locales that figure in the
narrative, all names, characters, places and incidences are the
products of the author's imagination or are used factiously. Any
resemblance to current events or locales, or to living persons, is
entirely coincidental.

Designer: Christine McCall
Editor: John Hough
Photo: John Lankes

LCCN: 2013922215

ISBN 978-0-9911973-0-9
eISBN 978-0-9911973-1-6

ACKNOWLEDGMENTS

This book could not have been written without the help of several people.

Thanks to–

Julaina Kleist-Corwin who mentors and inspires budding authors.

My monthly critique group who help me keep it real; Vee Byram, Neva Hodges, Lani Longshore, Julie Royce and Violet Carr Moore, who also did a superb final edit.

My beta readers whose feedback was invaluable: Michele Buckett, George Cramer, Nancy Nixon; and extra special thanks to Sheryl Shaeffer who read and re-read and re-read my manuscript.

My editor John Hough who was an enormous help in style, shape and suggestions to improve my story.

Christine McCall who produced a fabulous cover art and was a joy to work with.

Lastly, to the California Writers Club Tri-Valley Branch members who together nurture and support writers of all genres and levels.

RED ASSCHER
Living in Fear

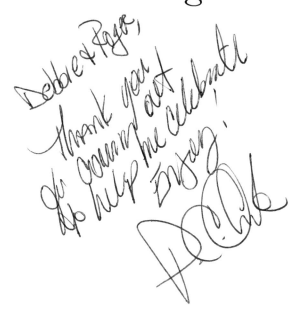

A Question
of
Belief

Some say a ring around the moon signifies a tempest. Some say a full moon releases shape-shifters, werewolves, witches, and monsters. Some tell tales of great misfortune and endless sorrow when a ring surrounds a Hunter's Moon.

ONE

Shanghai 1920

A HUNTER'S MOON, low in the sky, held an amber rim around its edge that night. The usual winds had vanished, replaced by an arid stillness. No one seemed to notice.

Swarms of people, cars, bicycles, and rickshaws scurried about like crazed jackrabbits. The smells of sweet steamed buns, reeking fish, and pungent congee from street vendors permeated the air. A wave of excitement ignited mystic Shanghai.

Foreigners to this land, a round-eyed man and woman dressed in formal attire stood on a street corner. They surveyed the exotic strangers that surrounded them.

Roman brushed his wife's auburn bangs to one side, stroked her cheek, and murmured, "It's good we are all together again."

"You were missed beyond measure," Kira replied.

The traffic guard raised his white gloved hand to stop motorists and bikers, with his other hand he waved pedestrians to cross. Roman and Kira sprinted across the road. One disobedient cyclist nearly clipped Roman.

"We must hurry," she said.

Roman tried to catch his breath. "Please . . . slow. . . down."

"Sorry my dear. I forgot about your old injury." She steered him down a narrow darkened alley. "It's a shortcut."

Halfway down the alley, the ground beneath their feet seemed to liquefy. They swayed unsteady on their feet. Kira grabbed her husband's arm for support. They could not walk, they could not run, they could not hide.

In the distance, they heard brick and mortar and window glass snap then crash to the ground. A loud crack overhead caused Roman to push Kira to safety before falling debris engulfed him.

The earth once again lay still. Deafening moans and cries reverberated throughout the city.

She rushed to her husband's side. "Help us. Someone, please help us." She cradled his head in her lap. He moaned, as his legs lay pinned under the rubble of brick and timber. Her tears fell onto his forehead. She stroked his ashen cheek.

"It will be all right. Hush my love, someone will come soon." She wadded up her wrap, to make a pillow then rose and hurried for help.

An oriental man, not much taller than Kira, dressed in a black cloak and black fedora, slithered out of the shadows. He walked with a cane, yet had no sign of a limp.

The woman shrunk back from the coldness of his manner but quelled her fear. "Please kind sir, it's my husband. I need to get him to a hospital." She ushered the stranger to her husband's side.

He knelt and studied the man. His lips formed a razor thin smile then he whispered. "You didn't think we'd let you live, did you?"

Roman tried to recoil but he was unable to move. His eyes darted around in search of Kira.

A lone bulb that hung above a cobalt blue painted door from across the way cast a flash of light onto the metal object withdrawn from the cane. The man plunged the blade into Roman's heart with a hard twist. A single gasp of air left the trapped body.

"Oh God," Kira cried out. Her face twisted in horror. She stared into the cold opaque eyes of the murderer. "Why? Why? Why?"

"It's what I do," he hissed and then thrust the knife deep into her body.

Kira shivered and mumbled, "Anya," then closed her eyes. The wheeze of death's rattle passed her lips.

The assassin wiped the bloodstained knife clean on the woman's green taffeta dress and slipped it back into the cane. A spark from her hand caught his attention. Upon close inspection, he saw a red stoned ring. He snatched it off her finger then stole away into the darkness.

The moon illuminated the wreckage, the pools of blood, the lifeless bodies.

Across town, a young woman waited in the hotel lobby for parents who never arrived.

TWO

San Francisco 1943

I SOLATED IN A sterile dingy gray room with little ventilation, Anya Pavlovitch had grown accustomed to the claustrophobic windowless cement walls. In many ways, she preferred the quiet confinement to the turmoil outside. Her eyes fixed, her ears attentive, her thoughts rhythmic with the tempo of the teleprinter as it spat cryptic letters onto white paper.

A jolt rocked the room and the light fixtures swayed above her head. A sudden queasiness churned in the pit of her stomach and saliva filled her mouth. She forced down the rancid taste of a Woolworth's Spam lunch special that bubbled up in her throat. She was accustomed to the frequent mild earthquakes that plagued this city. But with them, came solemn memories of her parents.

It's ironic, she shook her head, *I'd end up in a place prone to earthquakes. The gods can be cruel.* She bit the inside of her cheek and rubbed her finger where once a ring lay. *It's hard to remember the last time I was truly happy.* She tried to push away thoughts of her past. *It's not easy being a foreigner in a new land. I miss my mother country. I miss my childlike innocence. I miss my mamma and papa.* She buried her face in her hands.

The click, clack of the teleprinter ceased. She took a deep breath and cast off her sadness, regained her composure, and then removed the completed message.

```
DRAUGHT CONTINUES CC FROM G²
ACTION X EXCITING NEWS
WEATHER CLOUDY NEED UMBRELLA
CANT FIND ANYWHERE RR NEED
ASSISTANCE
```

Anya deleted the padded information before the X, leaving the classified information for decrypting. She reached for the latest codebook that allowed her to decipher and transcribe the true message. The process was laborious, but the challenge occupied her mind, which helped to squeeze out painful memories.

Anya's main assignment at the Office of War Information was to translate propaganda into Chinese and Japanese. Pamphlets bolstered American kindness and the cruelty of the Japanese leadership. Air support would then distribute them across Asia. The idea was to encourage Chinese guerrilla forces to further undermine the Japanese in China and dissuade Japanese sentiment throughout Japan's countryside. However, today's assignment was to translate a message that came in from an agent in the Far East.

Anya hurried to complete her final task so she could start her weekend. She marched to the office of her director with the memo in hand. Careful to knock before she opened the door, she spotted Edmund Atwater at his desk deliberating over his paperwork. He was a middle-aged, stout man with a patch of mahogany brown hair on the top of his head and long thick bushy eyebrows that touched his eyelashes.

She entered the dark wood-paneled room that offered a panoramic view of the newly constructed Golden Gate Bridge. The fog had lifted and just past Alcatraz Island, a merchant ship drifted out to sea. Not religious, she nevertheless, muttered a little prayer for its protection from submarine assaults.

She placed the decoded message in front of Atwater to make sure he focused on the memo.

> 3 January 1943
> Office of War Information
> Atwater's eyes only
>
> Have vital information. Under surveillance.
> No one trustworthy. Need assistance.
> – G²

Anya turned to leave the room and thought she heard a gasp from Edmund Atwater, then he cleared his throat. "You lived in Shanghai, didn't you Miss Pavlovitch?"

A cold sweat rushed through her body as she stopped short of the door. Her back to him she replied, "Yes sir," then spun around. "My family and I fled there after the Bolshevik revolution."

He rose from his desk. "Please, have a seat." He motioned her to one of the overstuffed armchairs positioned alongside the window. "Would you care for coffee?"

She obviously craved a cup but could not bring herself to accept. Biting her lower lip she said, "No thank you, sir."

She sat, legs crossed at the ankles like her mother had shown her, and watched him pour coffee from a silver urn. He slurped each steamy sip, which provoked her. She fidgeted in her seat in hopes he would again offer her a cup.

"Are you sure you wouldn't care for some?" he said.

"Well, if you insist." After all, she didn't want to offend him.

"Cream or sugar?" He cast a smile in her direction.

"Black is fine, thank you." She rubbed her naked ring finger. Although she no longer possessed the ring, it had become a reflex to the memory of her parents.

Atwater sat in the chair opposite her and hiked one leg over the other. "Miss Pavlovitch, you have been with OWI for a couple of months in our translation division. Is that right?"

"Yes, sir." In actuality, it had been well over six months since she had answered an ambiguous ad in the newspaper for a translator.

"I believe you know William Donovan, Director of Office of Strategic Services," he said.

Anya squirmed in her chair. "I know of him. My papa met him years ago when Mr. Donovan was in Omsk. The U.S. government tried to support Admiral Kolchak's overthrow of the Bolsheviks."

"Yes, too bad about Kolchak's murder. Did you know that Donovan was on his honeymoon when he was asked to go to Omsk?" He chuckled, "Mrs. Donovan must be a very understanding woman."

She lent a polite smile and lowered her jade green eyes. Just over forty, she was lucky her Titian red hair had not turned that dull twisted gray resembling most women her age. Her petite features and complexion similar to vanilla ice cream gave her an air of youthfulness, even though the wrinkles at the corners of her eyes stood out.

"Donovan is sending us a naval intelligence officer next week. I—we would like you to assist him," he said.

Anya wiped the perspiration from her palms on her plaid skirt. She picked up the coffee, took a sip, and swallowed hard. She shuddered to think what his next sentence might be.

"I want to encourage you to take a temporary assignment to Shanghai."

She felt the blood rush from her face. *Oh God, I*

can't go back there. Her legs quivered and caused the cup to rattle in its saucer. "Does this have to do with the memo?"

The corners of his mouth tilted up. "You would travel as a cultural attaché to a businessman." Atwater's eyebrows furrowed into one, giving him the appearance of a brute. "I won't discount the fact this could be dangerous. We know Shanghai is occupied by the Japanese but so far only minor incidents have occurred."

"What would be expected of me?"

"The usual, monitor chatter on the radio, assist the agent around the city, and support him with special requests."

"Oh . . . um." She twisted her ring finger harder until it turned bright red.

"You seem a bit apprehensive, Miss Pavlovitch. Is there something wrong?" Anya continued to fidget. She felt her throat close as he studied her.

"Oh yes," he said. "Your parents died in Shanghai. Earthquake wasn't it?"

"Missing," Anya muttered. She still could not come to terms with saying or hearing the word dead out loud. In the back of her mind was always a glimmer of hope she would one day find them. She looked down to see she had scrunched her skirt. "Their bodies were never recovered." She straightened the wrinkles.

"Yes, of course. I know it's a lot to ask of you. You don't need to give me your answer today but I will need a response by early next week."

She put her cup on the table nearby. They stood simultaneously. "Thank you, Mr. Atwater, for your confidence. I will give it great consideration."

"Thank you, Miss Pavlovitch. You know, you are my only choice for this assignment. It speaks well of the trust I have, given the short amount of time you've been with us." He rested his hand on her shoulder.

She felt as though her spine had collapsed from the weight of his hand.

"These are hard times when everyone needs to sacrifice," he said.

Anya bit the inside of her cheek, smiled, and tried to regain her backbone. She was not prepared to return to Shanghai and confront the possible truth about her parents. And what would Paval say?

.

THREE

Winter's fog shrouded Russian Hill. Anya's thighs ached from the arduous climb up the 168 Broadway steps then the four zigzag flights up the Florence steps. She wished instead that she had hopped on the Hyde cable car that ran by her flat. At the top, she gulped a mouthful of air, wiped droplets of mist from her nose, and faced the cityscape to catch her breath.

From her perch, she saw all the way down Broadway Street to the Bay. The bright lights made the city sparkle and the distance hid the knowledge of the prostitution that subsisted below.

Anya continued her trek in a state of oblivion with thoughts of Edmund Atwater's request and her Shanghai past muddled together. She had gone several blocks off her regular route when she turned down an unfamiliar street. She passed a red painted iron-gate embroiled with Chinese coins on each section. It triggered a memory of the house in Shanghai she and her parents had lived in with the same symbol. A sardonic laugh escaped her lips at the absurdity of its failed power to render prosperity and longevity. A sudden, almost electric sensation hit her hard, as though something had moved through her body. It unnerved her and she picked up her pace towards home.

Anya yelled up from the inside stairwell to their Edwardian flat. "*Pasha, ya doma, ti est.*" She continued up the stairs to find Paval at his desk. She stood silent and watched smoke billow upward from an unseen cigarette. Deep into his writing, even her bellow had not disturbed him. She hung her wrap on the oak hall tree, shuffled into the kitchen, put on her apron, removed beets from the icebox, and began to prepare the evening meal.

Anya sat at the tiny chalk white wooden kitchen table that held only enough room for two chairs. She studied the man across from her. The deep creases in his shirt looked as though he had slept in it for days. His gray matted mane and gaunt face added years to his pasty complexion. Anya sighed; *he could be mistaken for one of many invisible homeless who littered the vast countryside.*

Paval Vrubel, already well into his sixties and, although a published poet, was not well known. Fame, if it were to come, would be posthumous.

He appears more relaxed this evening, Anya thought. She had observed that this once gentle soul seemed agitated and quick to flare up in recent days. And he drank too much.

"Paval, today at work." She stopped.

"What?" He looked up from his meal.

"Nothing, it's not important." She sank in her chair with slumped shoulders. She straightened the green and white gingham kitchen curtains next to her then stared out the window into the night.

Paval slurped his soup and said, "The borscht is excellent." He used the spoon to pick up drops from his chin. He tore off a piece of bread, dipped it into his bowl, popped it into his mouth, and then threw back a swig of vodka from a jelly jar.

Anya's mind leaped back to when they first met. Eight years seemed like a lifetime ago but at that time, she ached for solace. She had discovered a book of his poems in a local bookstore. His verses articulated her sense of isolation and loneliness as a Russian refugee. It was an exceptionally dreary night when she had decided to rally herself and attend one of Paval's recitals. His dark eyes imparted the pain and torment his poetry expressed. Although twenty years her senior, she felt drawn to his eccentric manner.

It took all of her courage to speak to him. "Your expressions are equal to Pushkin." She tilted her head to one side and smiled. "*The Silent Russian* is my favorite." His hypnotic stare made her want to flee but she returned his gaze.

He said, "What part of Russia are you from?" His voice carried the quality of a baritone, rhythmic and serene.

"I'm a Muscovite but I spent my formative years in Vladivostok off the Sea of Japan," she replied.

"What's your name?"

"Anya Pavlovitch."

He looked at her with the surprise of a young child. "Are you any relation to Roman Pavlovitch?"

"Papa? Did you know him?"

Anya noticed Paval's eyes dart sideways and his cheeks glowed. He rubbed a twitch away in his left eye and said, "Every Russian knew of Colonel Pavlovitch. He and Admiral Kolchak were heroes to the people of Omsk."

Her Russian blood ran warm with pride. Something about this man, who resembled Ichabod Crane, endeared her to him.

That night Paval had invited her to join him and his friends for a late dinner. They reminisced about their lives in Russia and their disdain for the Reds.

Paval seemed inquisitive in regards to her father and asked about his escape to Shanghai. How she felt when they were all reunited. All painful subjects because they had not been together that long when the earthquake took her parents. His fascination with her father's memory charmed her and by the end of the evening, her infatuation had bloomed into true affection, although she never attained ardent love.

Although Paval guzzled vodka, was unkempt, and never seemed to see the virtuous side of life, Anya sensed a simpatico with him and resigned herself that poets have the right to brood. She cared for him, she nurtured him, she tried to heal him.

"Anya? Anya?" Paval waved his hand in front of her face.

Caught in her daydream, Anya blurted out. "Did you remember it's ladies night?"

Paval rose from the table and shot her a look of disapproval. She remained silent, ignoring his contempt. The narrow kitchen did not provide much room but Anya managed to scoot passed Paval to the counter where she poured distilled potato vodka into empty fruit jars. Her vodka could not compare to the sips she got from her father's glass as a child, but it would be good enough for the girls.

Paval came from behind and wrapped his arms

around Anya's waist then nuzzled his chin in the crook of her neck. She tried to pull away. "That tickles." She laughed and placed the jar on the counter. "You're going to make me spill."

He spun her around and kissed her. His hand moved to her breast. Anya stopped his hand when she heard someone clear their throat. They both looked over to see Virginia.

"The baby is sleeping," Virginia said, hand to her hip.

Anya straightened her apron and patted her hair back in place. She stared at Paval whose neck resembled that of a flamingo. He squeezed her hand and whispered, "I'll see you later."

The women's prattle agitated Paval so he agreed to watch Virginia's baby in her apartment. There was no fondness for the infant. It slept while he wrote in peace.

"You know we had that baby to keep my husband out of the military, but the draft got him anyway," Virginia said.

Anya smiled. "Yes, I know. Can you please take the kitchen chairs into the living room?"

Virginia, a buxom brunette with an aquiline nose, lived downstairs. Anya being petite and refined was the opposite of Virginia's tall and brash demeanor. Both worked at OWI and were inseparable, to Paval's dismay.

"I hear some of the girls on the stairwell. I'll go let them in," Virginia said.

Seven giddy women in a small apartment made it a struggle to move around more than a few feet in either direction.

"Does everyone have a drink? If not the vodka's in the kitchen," Virginia said.

"Okay, ladies let's start the meeting." Anya said. "I received enough ration coins from everyone to purchase a bag of sugar." Cheers erupted. "It's not as much as last month because we've lost a few of our members due to military relocations. I will divide equal shares into the jelly jars you each brought. That's it unless anyone else has something to say. No—okay then, meeting adjourned."

The thunderous music and shrill voices shook the walls as the vodka flowed. The fact that all of the neighbors were at Anya's left no one to call the cops when the noise got too loud; however, they were mindful of the dim-out regulation and secured the windows with blankets.

A myriad of conversations flew around the room when someone new burst onto the scene. "Did you hear? Lucy Abe in 8B has been taken to an internment camp somewhere in Arizona."

"Oh my."

"Honest?"

"Poor soul."

"Yeah, they found out her grandma is Japanese," a voice exclaimed.

Jane spouted, "I knew it. She has those dark slanted eyes."

Anya frowned at Jane. "Did you know Lucy's husband, also of Japanese descent, is over in Germany?" Anya thought of the thousands of Americans of Japanese, German, and Italian descent who fought against their heritage. It made her heart ache as she remembered how her father had fought for his beloved Russia against his countrymen.

Apprehensive that the government might consider internment for other foreign refugees remained foremost in her thoughts. Her clearance gave her access to Washington's growing concern about Communism. Russian refugees were under particular suspicion from special interest groups. She assured herself that as long as she remained valuable at OWI she and Paval would be safe. *But how safe can anyone be in these uncertain times?*

Anya's reprimand caused Jane's cheeks to flash red blotches. The voices quieted and the only sound heard was the song, *Paper Doll* on the radio.

Someone piped up. "I hear Frank Sinatra may come to town. But this time without Tommy Dorsey. I guess Sinatra's gone solo."

Coos permeated the room and once again, the

noise level returned to its fevered pitch.

ANYA HAD A slight headache and a severe case of anxiety the next morning. In less than thirty-six hours she would have to face Edmund Atwater. She marshaled her fears and decided to work in her garden. Gardening gave her the outlet to bend her consciousness back to a peaceful place.

Bundled in winter garb, Anya walked down the street with the warmth of the sun on her face. She jumped when a feral tabby cat darted out from under the bushes. She laughed at her skittishness. The cling, clang of the cable car bell rang and the conductor waved as he sped past her. She waved back then filled her lungs with the crisp fresh air and thought, what a perfect day.

Anya arrived at the garden plot half past one. Several co-op gardeners where already busy turning over the ground.

Fresh vegetables were in short supply and several neighbors had taken over a vacant lot. The government's propaganda made it clear that every American should be self-sufficient. And their Victory Garden was the best in the city, stated the San Francisco Examiner. One of the co-op tenants built a makeshift greenhouse that yielded select fresh vegetables year round.

Anya had had no idea about horticulture, or for that matter, what a rhubarb plant looked like. But over time she found herself with quite a green thumb.

While on her hands and knees, dirt up to her elbows in search of potatoes, her mind crossed over to Atwater's request. She felt a black cloud of doom take hold.

I can't go to Shanghai . . . and I wouldn't be any use to them if I did.

But if I don't go who will? It's not my problem. He'll have to find somebody else.

But I need to confront my fears. I can't live this way.

But I won't leave Paval, he needs me.

Anya sat back on her legs. "I'll just have to tell Mr. Atwater no, on Monday."

FOUR
Washington D.C.

D IGNITARIES AND SPECIAL guests crowded the stately room. The scent of mineral oil lingered from the freshly polished oval table. Those who could not find a seat, leaned against the back wall. Center stage hung the Presidential seal and to the left stood the proud Stars and Stripes. The noise level retreated as the speaker approached the podium.

"Good morning gentlemen," Commander Macdonald "Mac" Benson said as he adjusted his Windsor in his full dress naval uniform. His palms clammy and damp, nevertheless, he remained poised before the Joint Chiefs of Staff.

"Although Russia is a current ally, we still find it necessary to monitor the activities of Russians that live in the United States. The investigation continues of scientists and other personnel who possess certain scientific or political information in association with top schools, such as the University of Chicago and University of California Berkeley." Mac raised his head and observed several nods. "There are some scientists who feel it is important that no single country dominates the globe. Therefore, to create a balance of power they will share their research," he paused then directed his gaze at the audience. "Tell that to the Germans."

A spontaneous roar of applause erupted. Mac beamed and continued with his report.

When the meeting adjourned, a husky man with brushed backed silver hair approach Mac. The fellow had an impish smirk that lent a twinkle to his light blue eyes. He appeared a few inches shorter than Mac's six-foot two-inch frame.

The gentleman extended his right hand. "Good briefing, Commander. God willing, we will all come out of this war better for it." He slapped Mac on the shoulder. "Let me introduce myself, I am…"

"William Donovan," Mac said. "One doesn't get very far in this business without recognizing William Donovan."

Donovan said, "I'm told you are a graduate of the Naval War College."

Mac straightened as if someone had shouted attention. "Yes, sir . . . Class of '35."

"Do you know Kevin Jones?"

"Yes sir, Jonzy and I were bunk mates at the academy," Mac said.

"Kevin senior and I started out in boot camp together. Kevin's my godson." Donovan smiled as if he had something on Mac. "I'd like to get together. My office, say 1600 hours."

"May I ask what this is about, sir?" Mac said.

"I've got a tactical operation underway and I think you might be a good fit." Donovan's wide grin showed his tobacco-stained teeth.

Mac watched as the man with the golden tongue, known as "Wild Bill," walked away. Everyone knew of Donovan's reputation; accustomed to command, energetic, and not without ambition. All the characteristics Mac admired and believed made a great leader.

MAC ENTERED DONOVAN'S office at 1555 hours. It overlooked Pennsylvania Avenue and the rush from the traffic below provided a constant buzz. The room held a clean modest décor. A wooden desk faced the door with a floor to ceiling world map hung behind. Bookcases surrounded the walls with stacks of civil and military law books.

Sunbeams shot through the blinds revealing a pale blue haze. The pungent odor of stale cigarettes filled Mac's nostrils, and left a bitter taste in his mouth. A pile of mangled butts filled a tarnished ashtray and a pack of Lucky Strikes lay to Donovan's right. Mac stood at attention as Donovan lit up a fresh cigarette.

"At ease Commander, please sit down." Smoke billowed past his lips. "Cig?"

Mac replied, "No thank you, I'm a pipe man." Mac sat in one of the two chairs in front of the desk.

"You and General MacArthur," Donovan said. They both chuckled.

"Have a nip?" Donovan pulled out a bottle of Peter Dawson Scotch and poured a splash in two glasses. "To God and to country and to the annihilation of our enemies."

Mac tried to suppress a cough as the scotch burned down his gullet. He preferred the smoothness of a good Kentucky bourbon.

Donovan looked down at the folder in front of him, shifted his eyes over the top of his glasses. "I've read your dossier."

Mac felt his Adam's apple bob as he swallowed. The outcome from his last international assignment had gone awry. It caused his reassignment back to the States and the confinement of a desk job that he hated. He would take anything if it meant the opportunity to regain the freedom of field time.

"There is a small group that FDR put together

about six months ago that I think would suit your talents," Donovan said.

Mac had heard rumors about a new top-secret organization known as the OSS and he wanted in.

"Our role here is to collect and analyze strategic intelligence for the Joint Chiefs." Donovan took another puff on his cigarette. "Your file states that after graduation you spent time in Germany."

"Yes sir, I left for Germany in '37 and spent two years posing as a *Time* reporter gathering information about the Nazi Party."

Donovan said, "I see you also did a stint in England."

Mac lowered his eyes for a moment then returned his gaze. "Yes sir, the British military requested that I help them infiltrate German Intelligence. I posed as a U.S. government official with fanatical pro-Nazi beliefs who traveled to London on official business. I worked with several Nazi agents and passed on false information."

"I understand you ran up against some kind of trouble with one of your sub-agents. But I am confident the experience lent you a valued lesson."

Mac's heart took a flip-flop but his face remained expressionless. "Her death was unfortunate but my hand was forced."

Donovan slammed his fist on the desk. "That's why we need men like you, who care little about convention and will sacrifice anything for his country." Donovan poured another splash in each of their glasses. They both drank up.

"We need to get control of a landing strip in China to land aircraft, along with their security forces. This valuable real estate could end the war with Japan within a year. I need someone to travel to Shanghai and make a connection." He leaned in. "It's a dangerous and sensitive mission–with slight probability of success." Donovan sat back in his chair and studied Mac.

Mac's lapis blue eyes blazed. He was like an addict waiting for a fix. He needed this job to regain his standing in covert operations.

Donovan pushed away from the desk and rose. "I need you to get back to me tomorrow. Sorry for the short notice, but time is not a luxury we have, son."

Stimulated and not from the alcohol, Mac walked out overwhelmed but exhilarated. Outside a slap of cold air brought him around and for the first time since Donovan had approached him, his thoughts centered on his wife and young daughter.

FIVE

MAC STOOD STILTED in their monochromatic living room, which Helen had decorated. Two table lamps stood balanced on either side of a vanilla colored davenport that faced a white stoned fireplace. An oval coffee table rested on an oatmeal colored Berber area rug. Week-old Christmas decorations adorned the mantel.

Mac and Helen loved their brownstone in Georgetown, near the university. They had, by all standards of their family and friends, an idyllic marriage. However, recently he felt detached, an outsider, as though his family were distancing themselves.

Helen, still in her twenties, had curls of natural platinum blonde hair that brushed her shoulders. She donned a tawny brown dress cinched at the waist that emphasis her ample breasts. When she turned, the flare of her skirt twirled about her. "In the two years we've been married, I've seen you a total of maybe a month." Piercing violet eyes stared him down. "Why the hell did you marry me if you weren't going to stick around?"

"Because you got pregnant." Mac tried to catch his words but it was too late. His fingers sliced through his thick head of chestnut brown hair and tugged at the roots.

"I suppose you didn't have anything do to with that." Her hands clenched at her hips as she tapped her raven black Mary-Jane's on the wood floor. "What the hell am I suppose to do while you're gone?"

"You could go stay with your mother." He paced around the room like a trapped animal.

"That's your answer for everything. Go visit my mother."

Mac stopped and flailed his arms. "I told you before we got married that my job would involve travel. You didn't seem to mind then."

Helen exhaled. "We've discussed your taking a permanent desk job, why haven't you pursued that end?"

"Because it would hinder my career with Naval Intelligence."

"Your career. What about your daughter? She barely knows who you are," she said. "Do you even care to see her grow up?"

Mac tugged on a cowlick near his temple.

She crossed her arms at her chest. "You selfish bastard."

Both were locked in silence, neither willing to submit until Helen said, "Fine, go off and abandon us. I'll go to my mother's." She stomped upstairs and slammed the door shut.

Mac felt a pull to go after her but he knew no words to soothe her wrath. *If I go up there, she'll cry and persuade me to stay. I'd rather jump out of a plane without a parachute, pour gasoline over myself and light a match, or sit bare ass naked on a Texas red ant hill than refuse this assignment.*

MAC SAT AND waited while a middle-aged woman with horn-rimmed glasses loomed over William Donovan. He watched Donovan's pen bounce around as he signed each document without question. Mac pondered what exotic adventures he might encounter on his assignment.

"Thank you Miss Finch," Donovan said. He waited until she closed the door behind her before he spoke.

"China has been at war with Japan since '37, which is when this world war began. It's only since

Pearl Harbor that we've gotten involved."

Mac nodded.

Donovan continued, "As I said, this assignment will take you to Shanghai. It's an international city at the mouth of the Yangtze River. It's currently occupied by the Japanese and slithering with spies." Donovan scratched the gray stubble on his chin. "You see—we spy on the Chinese, the Chinese spy on the English and everyone spies on the Japanese. Then of course there are the French." He shook his head in disgust. "The French Concession, in Shanghai, has come under the rule of the Vichy Government. They're basically puppets for the Germans, which makes the French dangerous allies. I'm afraid they can't be trusted but then, no one can."

Mac was unfamiliar with that part of the world. His blood ran hot at the thought of unscrupulous characters and corruption that dominated the Far East landscape.

"We've tried to meet with General Chiang Kai-shek but his adviser, Dai Li, has blocked our every move." Donovan passed a photo of Dai to Mac. "He's known to many as the Himmler of China. That's him in the middle."

The black and white photo displayed a group of Chinese officers. Dai's diminished hairline gave him the appearance of a much older man. His eyes were set far apart with pronounced eyebrows, and he had a thick flat nose. "He does have a look of evilness about him."

"Li holds the title of Director of Investigation and Statistics. In actuality, he commands a combined secret police and intelligence organization. He parades around the countryside in his green train like General Patton inspecting his troops in a M46 tank." Donovan took a final drag of his cigarette, rubbed it out and continued. "He's rumored to have acquired vast wealth through the control of the opium trade."

Mac put his fist to his mouth and coughed from the smoke. "That may be something we can use to our advantage."

"Yes, and as for Generalissimo—he may be China's most powerful leader, but to us he's no more than a glorified warlord. Corruption is rampant in his organization. We believe he's in negotiations with Japan on a new treaty."

"Is it possible for us to reach our goal without Li?" Mac said.

Donovan smiled. "We need Chiang's support but Li's influence over him is daunting. He is a trusted protector of the General, so we need him in our corner or out of the picture altogether. We can't underestimate this man's cunning ways. We've learned that Li's men have developed poison tablets in the form of Bayer aspirin."

A cold shiver crawled up Mac's spine.

"We've also learned from the British not to misjudge Li's hold. When the Brits tried to organize a guerrilla force, Dai Li demanded that one of his men have complete power of the operation. And when the British ambassador went to the General to protest, Chiang refused to see him." Donovan waggled his forefinger. "You pay if you don't play with Li." They both laughed.

Donovan stood behind his desk and with a wooden pointer tapped on a world map. "China is an ideal launching pad for military strikes against the Japanese. If we can infiltrate behind enemy lines here in China, we can deploy troops and aircraft. If the Aussies move north through Indonesia while the English move east from India through Burma, we can position our forces from northern China and west from the Pacific. Together we can put a stranglehold on Japan's expansion and push her back home. But we need ground support from the Nationalists."

Mac thought, this is more of a critical mission than I had first imagined.

Donovan drew an imaginary circle around a group of islands. "The Japanese have a stronghold here in Saipan. Once we overtake this island, it would provide us with a strategic place to discharge B-29 bombers. I am not at liberty to discuss much more but suffice it to say, Saipan could play an important role."

Donavan lit another cigarette and exhaled. "Your assignment is to dig deep into the underbelly of Shanghai. Get close to their underworld. That will be the only way you can encounter Li." Smoke billowed out from his nose. "Li doesn't stay in one place very long. Our informants tell us Li will be in Shanghai several days after you arrive. We believe that Dai Li has outlived his usefulness. Use any means necessary to see this is accomplished."

Mac understood his assignment meant killing Li to develop closer negotiations with Chiang. His mind had clicked to honor, country, and duty. He would do whatever necessary to prove himself. "You mentioned the other day you wanted me to make contact with someone?"

"Yes, that would be Du Yu-seng, the head of a coldblooded gang in Shanghai. He is your best bet to get next to Li. If you're afraid of wolves, stay out of the forest."

Mac smiled. "Who will I be working with?"

Donovan opened a desk drawer and pulled out an airline ticket. He slid it across the desk. "You'll report to the OWI office in San Francisco. Edmund Atwater, the director there will set you up with travel plans. He'll have a package for you."

Mac wondered what he meant by package but

chose not to ask. If Donovan wanted him to know, he would have told him.

Donovan said, "We've arranged for you to work with our U.S. Consulate General's Office in Shanghai. Sheldon Henderson will be your contact. He's a straight shooter, all your needs will be met once you meet with him."

"Yes sir," Mac said. "I understand there's a threat of communist subversives in the area."

"The communist stronghold has become en-trenched and their current leader, Mao Zedong is building himself quite a peasant army. The British seem to look upon Mao as a more powerful ally than Chiang but we're not convinced. I don't know what's worse, the corruption in Chiang's regime or Mao's revolutionaries."

"I see what you mean." Mac rubbed his earlobe.

"I'm sending you into the fog. Remember, action is your sole objective and standard operating procedures may require less attention." Donovan stood and shook Mac's hand. "Good luck."

Mac cracked a faint smile and looked Donovan in the eye. "Thank you, sir. I won't let you down."

Mac made his way to the elevator. He pushed the down button and noticed his hand quiver. *Do I have what it takes to complete this mission?* He stood frozen for a moment. *Forget about London, that was years ago. Donovan knows about it and he still trusts I can get the job done.* Mac walked into the elevator and straightened his backbone. *This time my mission will be successful.*

He thought of Helen as the door closed. *I'll call her at her mother's when I reach San Francisco.*

SIX
China

THE FRANTIC HIGH-PITCHED shrieks squelched the rattle of dice against a forest green felt table. On the far side of the room, the *rat-ta-tat* echoed from a large revolving wheel. A pungent blue layer of smoke from cigarettes and cigars shrouded the area. A fat man at one of the tables let out a wet guttural cough and spat on the floor. It was morning and the gambling house had been at full tilt since dusk.

Sun Temujin shook the raindrops from his fedora and checked his damp belongings at the desk. He headed to a corner away from craps tables, roulette wheels, and mahjong players. His game of choice: Fan Tan, where he joined five men already seated.

At the center of the wooden table lay an etched

outline of a large square marked with the numbers one, two, three, and four on each side. The croupier placed a handful of dried shriveled beans at the center of the square and covered them with a porcelain bowl. Sun placed several coins on number one. The croupier motioned with his hand and all bets stopped. He removed the bowl and pulled four beans at a time with a bamboo stick. He continued the process until three beans remained on the table. No voices erupted, no gestures of congratulations, no celebratory signs emitted. The two stoic winners of number three fetched their winnings and the game resumed.

A dark-haired sultry woman in a mint green cheongsam beckoned Sun from across the way, but he dismissed her. His interest held for one thing and one thing only, the promise of a business venture.

A tap on his shoulder caused Sun to turn. "He's ready for you now," said a thin man sheathed in an ice white tunic and pants that ballooned out several inches from his legs. Sun picked up his remaining coins and the package he had laid at his feet. He followed the man down a darkened hall covered with yellow flocked wallpaper. Sun wiped his moist palms on his pants, choked back his trepidation, and opened the door.

Sun observed a modestly decorated room, a

reflection of its owner. Dai Li sat behind a large teak reddish-brown desk with simple carving on the sides and at the feet. His hairline receded three quarters of the way back from his forehead. His skin cast a pale hue and one eye drooped. Li wore an unembellished crisp blue tunic uniform with a high collar. To the untrained eye, he appeared simple, unassuming, but Dai Li was anything but ordinary.

Sun approached the desk with some trepidation. He understood the power this man wielded. "I am honored at your presence Major General Li. I bring this gift for your enjoyment." Sun bowed and placed the wrapped bottle of cognac on the table.

Li gave Sun a slight head bob and motioned for him to sit. A manservant poured hot tea for both men.

Sun saw Li's attention directed at the side of his face. Stares no longer fazed him. He had received a sizeable scar across the top of his hairline in a knife fight. The incident led him to become an expert knife handler, which raised his prominence in the underworld as a stealth assassin.

Li slurped his tea then spoke. "You play with fire Temujin."

The hairs on Sun's arms bristled and his stomach muscles constricted but he repressed any outward sign of emotion. To reveal fear would invite a bullet in the temple or a blade across the throat.

"I can't have you disrupting my plans with indiscriminant killings. No matter whose orders you are under." Li's voice never rose above a whisper. His body remained stationary. Hands visible, yet still. Eyes locked on Sun.

Sun knew Li had reason to want him dead. Sun had assassinated an agent that Li had planted in Mao Zedong's guerilla camp. But that had been several years ago when Sun had supported the communists, until their funds ran low. Now he wanted to align himself with people who had capital.

"I have summoned you here to redeem yourself," Li said. The servant refilled Li's cup, careful not to spill.

Sun remained silent and sat tall in his chair. His crossed leg started to tingle from an ailment he had acquired in the last several years.

"I have already lost one shipment at sea and can't afford to lose another." Li referred to opium. Everyone knew of Li's affiliation with the opium trade. Sun despised opium. He believed it a malignant blight on society. But he would overlook it because he more than craved this job, he needed it.

"I fill many pockets to see my operation runs

without incident. Reports from my partner in Shanghai are inconsistent. I've heard rumors there is a Hong Kong element trying to infiltrate our Shanghai trade. I need your eyes and ears down south."

Sun nodded. He bit the inside of his cheek to restrain the pleasure at his good fortune.

Li continued, "I am also suspicious of our American allies. They are not forthcoming with information to Generalissimo Chiang Kai-shek. We suspect the Yank's counter-intelligence might be making a ploy to take over our operation in an effort to gain untraceable monies to recruit double agents."

Sun's back ached and he sensed numbness in his right leg. He wiggled his toes to regain circulation and hoped the meeting would end soon. He did not care about the cause, just the objective.

"Someone has betrayed us and we need to find a crack in the traitor's armor and wedge a spear in it." Li handed a folder to the manservant who passed it to Sun.

Sun used the handoff to shift his position and stretch his back. He felt pinpricks like spiders crawling up his leg as the blood flowed once again.

"Someone has been sloppy and the pig needs castrating. The information in the file will assist you. We believe this person is working with the communists," Li said.

Sun smiled. This assignment offered more than that of a spy—it also called for an assassin.

"Take my train to Shanghai. I hope to follow in a couple of days. Things are a bit dicey around here and I need to remain on the move." Li waved his hand to signal the end of the meeting.

"Yes, Major General Li." Sun stood and bowed then retrieved his coat and cane.

THE RAIN ON Sun's face washed away a layer of smoke residue. He gasped for a breath of air then released his pent up emotions with a sigh. He had for the moment, eluded death.

Sun walked past a Buddhist temple said to hold some of the cremated remains of the Buddha. A five-tiered stone pagoda stood at the main gate. He thought about entering the temple but recognized, given his past deeds, his prayers would go unheeded.

He arrived at the rail station and made his way through the archway and down a tunnel. The foul order of urine made Sun quicken his steps. In the distance sat Li's personal locomotive, followed by two metal gray carriages. Sun stepped into the last car to find a less than posh interior. It held simple wood paneled walls with bench seats, table, and small kitchenette, typical of Li's modest taste.

Sun walked down the narrow aisle of the second carriage that held several sleeping compartments. The sleeper had two bunk beds, the upper one still locked in its upright position. On the lower bed lay a taupe colored blanket with a pillow propped against the wall. An adjoining washroom included a large container of hot water, slippers, and dressing gown.

Sun stripped off his clothes and slipped into the robe and slippers. He poured hot water into the basin and washed himself. He looked at his reflection in the mirror. Now in his early fifties, his reflexes and stamina were in decline. He knew he could no longer live the life of a mercenary, although he found it hard to give up the thrill of the kill. If successful with Li, he would be able to retire in comfort, but he had something set aside if things did not work out.

A knock came at the door. Sun opened it to see a manservant with a tray. Sun stepped aside and ushered him in. The sweet aroma of hot biscuits filled the room. The servant poured green tea into a porcelain cup then left without a word.

Sun's stomach growled. It had been over forty-eight hours since he last ate. He gobbled one, two, then three biscuits. The warmth of the beverage in his belly gurgled. He felt revitalized as he reached for the folder Li had given him. It contained the picture of a Caucasian man with light colored possibly, grey hair. He studied the face and smiled, "Lucky bastard, you have only twenty-four more hours to live."

SEVEN
San Francisco

E DMUND ATWATER EXTENDED his right hand to welcome Macdonald Benson. "Toss your hat and coat anywhere," Atwater said. "How was your flight?"

Mac had flown 3,000 miles aboard a military cargo aircraft. He had only managed to catch a few winks in the taxicab from the airport but he replied, "Fine, sir."

He threw his hat and coat over one chair and fell into the other.

"From what Donavan tells me, you're an indispensable man."

"I'd like to think I can hold my own if it comes down to it," Mac said.

"I'm not quite sure what your assignment is but if Donovan's involved, I'll bet it's covert." Atwater gave Mac a sly wink.

Mac stiffened. He was determined to make sure nothing passed his lips that would jeopardize his mission.

Atwater opened the folder on his leather-topped desk and rifled through the pages. "We have you scheduled to fly out at the end of the week. You will rendezvous with a ship at an un-disclosed island. From there you will make your way to Shanghai." Atwater leaned back and rested his arms on the chair's arms. "The Japanese have allowed a mercy ship to dock in Shanghai to collect foreign diplomats who've been caught up in this bloody war. We can get you into port," Atwater paused. "But we haven't quite figured out how to get you out."

"I'm sure I can manage."

"By the way, I have assigned you an OWI liaison."

Mac twisted his lips. "I prefer to work alone, sir."

Atwater tugged on his ear lobe. "I am afraid I'll have to insist on this Commander. I'll get you her dossier and arrange to have you speak with her tomorrow."

Mac frowned. "Her?"

"Is there a problem?"

"I guess not—as long as she has clearance."

Atwater leaned forward. "All employees are

given comprehensive background checks. And we continue periodic surveillance to monitor their activities."

"Of course, I didn't mean to suggest otherwise," Mac said.

Atwater relaxed his shoulders, cleared his throat, and continued, "I know it's a man's world, but sometimes you need a woman. Her lifestyle may not be what either you or I would consider respectable, but she is a valued asset. She knows things." He lifted one eyebrow. "Like the lay of the land. How things get done. Inside knowledge about Shanghai that neither you nor I possess."

Mac felt a sharp throb in his temples. *What the hell does a dame know? She'll be trouble. They always are.*

Atwater rose from his chair. "You must be exhausted after your flight. Why don't you go to your hotel and relax. I'll have my secretary arrange an office for you while you're with us."

"Thank you sir," Mac said and walked out the door. His teeth clenched and hands balled up. "Relax. I'm relaxed," he mumbled and quickened his pace down the hall.

EIGHT

ANYA RACED UP the office stairwell. She tripped on a step, but managed to grab the banister and save herself from a fall. Breathless, she flung open the stairwell door, took two steps then, wham. She had run into someone and landed on the floor with her legs spread-eagled.

Anya heard a man's voice. "Excuse me, Madam, but you need to slow down. You could hurt yourself."

She let out a muffled moan and picked herself up from the linoleum. The man tried to assist her but she slapped his hand away. Once on her feet, she straightened her skirt and checked the seams in her stockings. She sensed his pursuant eyes as she scurried away, but had too much on her mind to give him any consequence.

Anya marched into Edmund Atwater's office

ready to refuse the assignment to Shanghai. Atwater greeted her before she could utter a word. "Anya, I can't tell you how pleased we are that you have accepted the mission." He shook her hand with vigor then eased his grasp.

"But . . . but," she said.

"You are onboard?"

She had stood in front of the bathroom mirror the night before and practiced her refusal speech, but after all that self-posturing she could not find the courage to refuse. Her body slumped. "Yes, sir."

"The outcome of this undertaking is critical. I," he paused. "We all, rely on you."

A halfhearted smile crossed her face. "Thank you sir . . . I'll . . . 'll do my best."

"I know you'll make us proud," Atwater said. "Please have a seat. I'd offer some coffee but it's late in the day and it seems we're out."

"Quite all right, sir." Anya felt the warmth of the chair seat penetrate through her skirt. She wondered who had been here only a few minutes ago. Her cheeks flushed.

"You just missed Commander Benson, from OSS."

A scowl crossed Anya's face. She had been in too much of a hurry to get more than a glimpse of him. "Sorry sir, what did you say?"

"Commander Benson, he wants to meet with you."

"Me?" She sat up in her chair. "What about, sir?"

"He'll update you on your role. Not to worry, you'll both see the merits of each other's worth."

Anya's forehead wrinkled.

"Anya." Atwater's voice became firm like a drill sergeants. "You must rely on the Commander if you should get into any trouble. He's trained in self-defense and can aid in your success of the mission."

"Yes, sir." *God Almighty, what have I gotten myself into?* Anya slouched back in her chair, resigned to the fact that she had committed herself. "Sir, how long can I expect to be gone?"

"Several days travel then one week there. Shouldn't be more than a couple of weeks."

Egad, a couple of weeks. I guess Paval will just have to fend for himself.

NINE

PAVAL SAT AT the kitchen table and sipped his vodka from a jelly jar while Anya poured dish soap into the basin. His shaky voice muttered, "Why must you go? Don't go."

Anya turned to face him. "In each of our lifetimes we should all be forced to do the right thing. This is my time, my opportunity—I've given it careful thought." She lied.

"But why?"

Anya lowered her voice as though someone might hear them. "I shouldn't tell you this, but the current state of affairs in the Pacific doesn't look good. Half of the American fleet has been destroyed, leaving much of the air support grounded." She sauntered over to Paval and stroked his stubble cheek. "It's only for two weeks. I will be back before you can miss mc." She collected the turquoise Fiesta dinner plates from the table and returned to the sink. "I've made arrangements for Virginia to check in on you while I am away."

"That cow." He pressed the cool glass against his forehead. "You won't return."

Anya threw the dishrag into the washbasin. Soapsuds erupted. "Oh, stop it."

"I should have married you years ago, but it never seemed the right opportunity." He finished his drink and murmured, "With any luck I'll be dead by spring."

Anya rolled her eyes at his self-pity. "Virginia and I plan to see the new Bogart film, 'Casablanca' at the Alhambra. Do you want to join us?" She picked up the last spoons from the table and continued. "One of the *Thin Man* series is a double feature." Anya knew Paval fancied himself as a Nick Charles sort, sleuth, gambler, and booze guzzler. She had to admit he had the drinking part down pat.

Paval poured a splash of vodka into his empty jar. "*No mom Konfeta*, you two go—I need to write."

She crossed her arms at her chest. "Paval, you sit at your desk and write day and night. You should at least get out at night." Her voice started to develop that high-pitched sound when she got agitated. "I work, I garden, I have friends. But you, you're cooped up in this apartment all day." She hesitated then blurted out, "it's not healthy."

He slammed both hands on the table. Anya jumped and shrunk back. Although not quick-tempered, when provoked, Paval had a biting tongue.

"I go out," he snapped. "How do you know what I do when you are not here? Tell me that. Do you have your spies on me?" He gulped his vodka and refilled his jar to the rim.

Anya lowered her head and returned to the dishes. He made his way to her side and folded her petite hands into his own. He kissed her sudsy palms. "You go to the movies, I will finish up—go now," he waved her off.

Anya cast a mournful gaze in Paval's direction then turned to collect her hat and coat.

ANYA AND VIRGINIA walked down Green Street to the Alhambra Theater. The fog embraced them and a cold ocean breeze brushed their faces. Anya's mind wandered to Paval's down-trodden look before she left that evening.

Virginia pulled an envelope from her pocket-book. "I received a letter from Ray today." She waved it in front of Anya to gain her attention. "He wants me to come to Honolulu and bring the baby. He says he's lonely. Get this—the women tempt us in their tiny sarongs, come soon." She turned to Anya. "What the hell is a sarong?"

Anya shrugged her small shoulders.

"I'll blacken both his eyes if he thinks he can cheat on me." Virginia placed the folded letter in her coat pocket then locked her arm in Anya's.

They passed an elderly couple coming up the hill. The man pulled a metal cart filled with a bag of groceries.

"Good evening." They said in unison. The man tilted his hat as they passed.

"You seem upset," Virginia said. "What's troubling my little babushka?"

"It's Paval. He's so irritable. I feel something more than my leaving has him agitated. I can't seem to reach him. He's trying to drive me away with all these arguments about nonsense." She pulled her coat collar up around her neck. "I know in my heart he wants to reach out and tell me what's on his mind but his stubbornness gets in the way."

"I've never understood your relationship. He is so old. I don't mean in appearance, although that's evident, but in spirit. He's an old curmudgeon who mopes all day and waits for you to come home and fix his dinner. He has no friends, anyway not to my knowledge. Do you go anywhere together?"

Virginia stopped then Anya stopped.

"Where's the laughter in your life, Anya?'

Virginia said. "His suffering has become your misery."

Several cars whizzed by as they continued down the hill.

Virginia's words were harsh, but Anya had to admit there was an element of truth to them. It had been a long time since she had laughed. But in some regard she didn't feel she deserved happiness, not since her parents' disappearance.

"I appreciate your concern, but Paval and I share things you can't understand. Our lives have traveled over treacherous roads that cause one to withdraw. And yes, he broods, but he has cause to languish. He's a poet."

"Ah yes, that age old chestnut, like all writers are drunks," Virginia said.

Anya flashed Virginia a cold look. "Sometimes you have to search hard to find the good in someone. It may be the excessive drink, but I fear his mind's a bit muddled."

"Maybe you should take a trip up to Napa," Virginia said.

"He'd never agree to a vacation."

Virginia snickered. "No I mean the state asylum is up there." Virginia made a circular motion at her temple with her index finger. "You know, the house for the crazies. I'll be happy to give state's evidence."

Anya exhaled knowing she and Paval held little regard for each other. "I just need to get him out of the apartment but you'd think I wanted a pint of his Russian blood."

A black cat raced across their path. They looked at each other. "Bad luck," Virginia said.

"I don't believe in it," Anya replied then crossed herself.

"Why not go to the Palace of Fine Arts. The Impressionists are on display," Virginia said. "You know how much Paval enjoys that period."

Anya pondered for a moment then said, "Perfect." For the first time in days, Anya felt some relief as they walked into the movie house.

THE FOG HAD lifted early the next afternoon and Anya drank up the sun's warmth. She had gotten permission from Atwater to take Tuesday afternoon off. She hooked her arm in Paval's arm and they strolled passed the shops on Van Ness Avenue. She had gotten him out of the house without a struggle. He seemed keen on the idea, almost eager.

Paval stopped and kissed Anya on her temple. "It's a good day, the kind that allows you to forget the world's troubles."

"You're in such a good mood, so relaxed,

almost giddy," Anya said.

Paval whispered in her ear, "Let's go to City Hall and get married."

Anya's jaw dropped open. "Are you mad? I am leaving for the Far East at the end of the week. Besides, I believe you have to take a blood test or something."

Paval scowled then his face illuminated. "Then let's take the train to Reno tonight. We can return in the morning and no one will be the wiser."

"I . . . I." Anya stammered. "I'll be back in a few weeks then we can talk about a wedding." She stroked his cheek with her gloved hand and noticed his eyes had lost their glitter. In that moment, he seemed older, a weakened man. Her concern lay heavy on her heart at his relapse into morose sadness.

They spent the afternoon examining Van Gogh's *Irises*, Monet's *Haystacks*, and Renoir's portraits. Paval's usual commentary of the movement on canvas and broad patches of color was absent. He remained distant and when Anya tried to touch him, he ignored her.

On the walk home, Paval's demeanor had turned sluggish. He shuffled up the street in a daze.

"Maybe we should hail a cab?" Anya said. Paval continued to stagger up the street to the corner.

"Paval, stop." She pulled him back from the

honking horns from oncoming traffic. "Talk to me. What's the matter?"

She spotted a cab on the other side of the street and flagged it down. The cab driver motioned he would cross the street and pick them up.

She heard the roar of a bus. "Paval, step back from the curb." A flock of pigeons took flight and diverted her attention. She heard Paval mumble something. Then, as if in slow motion, Anya saw Paval's foot leave the curb as the vehicle sped towards him.

Her heart raced and she screamed, "Paval."

The sound of screeching tires came first followed by burning rubber, then a loud thud. Paval flew past her. He resembled a rag doll; arms and legs flailing. The bus skidded to a stop just shy of his limp body. Blood splatters permeated his torn clothing. A large crack in his skull exposed bits of brain.

Screams of horror floated all around her. The mummer of questions echoed, "Madam, are you all right? Madam. Madam . . ."

Anya stood frozen, mouth agape, body numb. Then everything went black.

TEN

PAVAL'S DEATH LEFT Anya with regret having agreed to take the Shanghai assignment. She vacillated over her decision. *The war effort needs me but I'm not certain I have the strength anymore. I must decline.*

She stared across the urban terrain from her apartment window. The late afternoon sky was clear with the exception of a single cloud in the west. Her long thick lashes still held the tears from an ardent cry. *They say that God gives you what you can handle. How much loss can I cope with in one life?*

The low setting rays of the sun caressed her body like a shroud. Anya longed to curl up like a cat on the wood floor and sleep forever. She wandered over to the bedroom closet and picked up a white dress shirt that lay crumpled on the floor, held it to her nose, and inhaled. The scent of tobacco and coffee still lingered. She dabbed her eyelashes dry with the shirt. *I'm not sure whom I pity, myself or the man who left me.*

Anya sat at Paval's desk and sank into the leather chair. The tips of her toes just touched the floor. She felt like a Lilliputian. Not allowed to sit at his writing table when he was alive, Anya felt uneasy yet consoled. With the flat of her hands, she rubbed along the grain of the oak wood on the only spot available. She surveyed the disheveled stacks of papers from unfinished manuscripts to poems that littered the room. A smile crossed her lips as she remembered his gray mane, rumpled attire, and the incessant cigarette smoke that billowed upward as he sat writing night after night after night.

She opened the bottom drawer and pulled out a bottle of vodka, poured a splash into a shot glass, held it up high, and looked to the heavens. "For all your pain and anguish, I hope now you will attain the fame you deserve. *Dasvidania.*" She downed the vodka and slammed the empty glass on the desk. The vibration caused a catawampus stack of papers to fall to the floor.

"Damn it."

Anya bent down to pick up the fallen pages. A folded piece of paper with her name in bold letters caught her attention. She unfolded a third of the paper, then stopped. She bit her bottom lip then opened it and laid it flat on the desktop. Both her hands covered the words; she closed her eyes for a second and inhaled. Then she removed her hands and read:

Anya Milaya Moya,

If you are reading this, then I am sorry to say I am no longer with you. It also means that you are sitting at my desk. I will talk to you about that later.

Anya filled her glass again. "Even in death, you can make me laugh, Paval."

I fear your judgment will be harsh after you read this letter. Please know that I love you as much as my heart can hold. Before I met you I was in a wasteland, alone and unsure of my destiny.

The truth is, I should have died in Russia.

The letter rattled from her trembling hand. The sudden recollection of what Paval had said before the bus hit him. *I should have died in Russia.* She squeezed her eyes shut at the memory. *Why didn't I see this?* She reached for her vodka, gulped it down, then refilled the glass.

You once asked me if I knew your father. Yes, I knew Colonel Roman Pavlovitch. I met him when he and Admiral Kolchak came to rid our homeland of those loathsome Bolsheviks. I wrote for a local paper that exposed the truth about Lenin. Your father and I spent many hours together. He spoke often of you and your mother. He loved you both very much.

By 1918 the Tsar loyalists had lost their spirit. Flocks

*of men deserted daily, due to starvation and discouragement.
Towards the end, there was not much of an army for
Kolchak and your father to command. Even the Americans
tried to assist but to no avail.*

*Forced to abandon their quest to save Mother Russia,
they retreated and planned to escape to Irkutsk then on to
Vladivostok, and finally to Shanghai.*

*I heard that the Bolsheviks arrested Kolchak in Irkutsk
and later executed him. I learned that your father had
escaped.*

*A man, Chinese I believe, desperate to find your father
contacted me. Festering pus would be the best way to describe
him. If you were to cut him, evil would ooze out.*

*Heavyhearted and with reluctance, I revealed your
father's location.*

Anya's hand jerked and knocked over the glass.
Vodka streamed across the writing table and onto
Paval's papers. *No that can't be true. I couldn't love a
traitor.*

She crushed the letter in her hand and
screamed, "Damn you to hell Paval," and threw it
to the floor.

Anya sopped up the liquid with the papers on
the desk and yelled at the chair. "You traitor—you
betrayed my papa, you betrayed your country, you
betrayed me. I will never forgive you." She threw
the glass against the wall. It shattered into pieces.

Anya rubbed her temples, tugged at her hair.

"How could I have been so blind . . . so stupid . . . not to see the evil in him."

"God—I wish I were dead."

She stomped into the bedroom and opened the window. Anya's upper body hung over the ledge. A blast of wind knocked her back into the room. She thrust herself out further. Halfway out, the skirt of her dress caught on the bottom windowsill lock. She looked down from the third-story window and thought, be smart Anya, he's not worth it.

She drew in a deep breath to calm her thumping heart but anger overwhelmed her. She sprinted to the closet pulled an armful of Paval's shirts, pants, and a single jacket off the rod, hangers still attached, then flung them out the window. She opened his drawer in the highboy, grabbed his underpants, undershirts, and socks, then threw them out too.

"I want everything about you out of my house," she shouted.

Next, she snatched his hairbrush off the dressing table. She grabbed the pack of his Chester-fields. She noticed a framed picture of the two of them. Anya recalled the pleasant summer day, years before the attack at Pearl Harbor. They had had a picnic with friends and talked about their good fortune in America. Both sat on a blanket, her legs tucked under a cotton dress while his legs stretched out with his torso turned towards her. He was in mid-sentence when the photo had been snapped.

Anya dropped his belongings and collapsed on the floor. She buried her face in the bed covers and beat her fist on the bed.

"Why? Why? Why?"

She gasped for air, staggered to the bathroom and splashed cold water on her swollen eyes. Exhausted, she prepared a cup of tea. Her mind numb, she found herself back at Paval's desk.

The crumpled letter lay at her feet. She flattened it out and took up reading where she had left off.

Anya, understand, my wife and two sons had been threatened.

Anya blinked several times and she shook her head. "Wait? What?" She reread the passage. He had never mentioned he had a family. She fought to remain calm, took a sip of tea, and continued.

The man said if I did not help him, he would have soldiers rape then kill my wife and slaughter my sons. I tried to hide my family, unfortunately, he found them and took them away. Agony will always be mine.

How I escaped and made it to America I do not remember or chose to forget. I felt like a tumor that needed to be cut from society but I could not find the courage.

Years later and halfway around the world there you were. I believed this was a sign of redemption, a chance to mend my wrong. I'm sorry I was not honest with you. I could not find the strength. The best of intentions can bring the greatest harm.

I know that you must be beside yourself at what you consider my disloyalty. And by now have gathered my papers to burn. Please accept I had no other choice offered to me.

My torment, though self-inflicted, has caused you to suffer. For that, I am sorry. I have lived in tragedy most of my life and I cannot remember how to live with happiness.

Forgive my craven behavior.

All my heart,

Paval

Anya placed the letter on the desktop and paused, quiet in her thoughts. *I'm not sure I can ever forgive you. I know the rational thing is to understand your dilemma but you dishonored my papa.*

She massaged the back of her neck. *And what of the Chinese man.*

"I know for certain, that I can't stay in this apartment . . . too many ghosts. I feel as though someone has my throat." She tugged on her collar. "I need a place to breathe."

Anya headed towards Union Street to the Italian district. The aroma of garlic, rosemary, and sausage from a plethora of restaurants permeated the air. Her belly growled, but she ignored the hunger pangs and strolled through the freshly mowed lawn of Washington Square Park. She stopped in front of St. Peter and Paul Cathedral.

The Cathedral's vivid white twin spirals rose to a majestic silhouette against a cerulean blue backdrop. She raised her head to the sky and thought, I wish I knew how to pray.

A shockwave ran through her body from the loud blast of a bus horn. Palpitations in her heart climbed to a crescendo and her stomach burned. *I don't want to live in agony like Paval and end up with my body mangled under a bus.*

Anya arrived at a point on the crest of a hill where she spotted a tugboat maneuvering a cargo ship towards the Golden Gate Bridge. She watched the ship until it drifted well past the bridge and headed out to sea. *I must cast off my timorous existence. I will be brave, I will be confident.*

"I will return to Shanghai."

ELEVEN

ANYA RODE UP in the elevator with a certain amount of trepidation. *Who was this Commander Benson and why did I need his approval? Mr. Atwater already said I'd been assigned.*

The doors parted, she stepped out onto a dingy and scuffed parquet floor. Several ceiling bulbs had burned out, which contributed to its grimness. A voice resounded from an opened door down the hall. She clicked-clacked her way down and peered inside the doorjamb, to see a man dressed in a blue naval uniform. He held a phone to his ear as he tapped a tobacco pipe against a metal wastebasket. She remembered her first encounter with this man and her face reddened.

"I don't know . . . yes . . . Helen . . . Helen, let's discuss it when I return. Okay . . . goodbye." He slammed the phone into its cradle.

Anya straightened her dark wool skirt and steadied herself one last time then cleared her throat to draw his attention.

Mac waved her to enter.

She advanced, leaving the door open.

The room resembled a storage area with file cabinets that bordered dreary gray walls and partially hid the windows. The morning sun peeked through the Venetian blinds. A metal desk and two folding chairs looked to have been plopped in the middle. On the table lay a phone, folder, and pitcher of water with glasses.

Mac rose from his seat. His height overshadowed her. The wideness of his azure eyes suggested his surprise and he burst into loud laughter. "You're the woman who tried to knock me down the other day." He swallowed his amusement as she drew near.

His laughter irritated her and she did not care for his blustery manner. She still felt vulnerable over Paval's death, and scrunched her shoulders with an embarrassed smile. Forced to lift her head high to meet his eyes she had an impulse to retreat but duty kept her feet glued in place. At close range, Anya thought he had a virile look with his high cheekbones and patrician nose. A cropped cowlick of chestnut hair near his left temple gave him a boyish appearance. She suspected he was a few years younger than she.

He motioned her to the chair in front of the desk. "Have a seat. I'm Commander Macdonald Benson." He sat, removed a pinch of tobacco from a red tin, and stuffed it into his pipe. He chuckled under his breath and said, "I understand we will be traveling together Miss Pavlovitch. May I call you Anya?"

I'd like to take the end of that pipe and poke it in your eye socket. That would put a halt to your amusement. She detested a man wearing the uniform whose behavior lacked manners befitting a military man. A military man should behave like her father, dignified and courteous.

"It's Ah-n-ya, soft 'a' at the start."

Mac cast an indifferent glance her way and lit his pipe. He drew several shallow puffs then expelled smoke. A sweet-spiced aroma filled the room. "Suppose you tell me a little about yourself."

She despised the interview process. Its only aim was to make one feel uncomfortable and put one on the spot, she thought. But she had no recourse other than to cooperate. She rubbed her finger and spoke, "I'm Russian by birth." She noticed his body tense and wondered if he disliked Russians. "Mamma and I escaped from the Bolsheviks to Shanghai while Papa joined the White Army, but it wasn't too long after when he joined us."

Mac had little expression except for a fixed gaze that made her hesitate for a moment. The folder on the desk made her suspicious about how much he knew about her. She continued, "I've been in America for over thirteen years. I'm fluent in Russian, Mandarin, Japanese, French, and English." She rested her hand on her knee to stop her crossed leg from swinging. "I have been with OWI in San Francisco for over six months. My most recent assignment has been to prepare propaganda information for dissemination on the Japanese mainland. I also monitor and log Japanese military radio transmissions."

"Do you have top secret clearance?"

Anya nodded.

"You seem nervous. You've rubbed your finger red and your leg seems to have a peculiar twitch. Do you think you are fit enough to make this trip?" he said.

She put her hands on her lap, planted both feet flat on the floor and looked at him head on. His mannerism made her arm and neck hairs bristle like an angry cat. She did not care for his abruptness. Not even Paval treated her with such disdain.

Mac leaned back in his chair. "I have to be honest—I'm not altogether pleased about taking a woman into a war-torn country. I may not always be there to protect you," he said.

"I can take care of myself, sir."

He snickered. "I'll have to trust you on your survivor skills." Mac chewed on the stem of his pipe.

What arrogance. He thinks I'm helpless or an idiot. She sensed his obvious contempt at the arrangement. Who was Helen, she wondered. "And you sir, are you leaving anyone behind?"

Mac fell forward with his pipe wedged between his teeth. "You're not here to ask questions but to obey my orders. Is that clear?"

His bark caused her to sit back in her chair.

A sudden spark then a small flame ignited from within the bowl of the pipe. Mac jerked the pipe from his lip and jumped up then dumped the burning tobacco into the wastebasket. He poured water from the pitcher into the basket, which emitted a sizzle, followed by a cloud of smoke. He put the pitcher down and sat unruffled.

Anya wanted to laugh but held it in. "What exactly are my duties, sir?"

"Well, we're not heading for a church social."

Anya felt an exasperated click escape from her tongue. *What a knucklehead. Does he think he's funny?*

Mac pulled on his collar and cleared his throat, "Some of the same things you do here, monitor radio transmissions, decipher messages, send updates to headquarters." He strummed his fingers on the desktop. "I understand that you have intimate knowledge of Shanghai."

She tugged on her skirt and repositioned her posture. "That was some time ago, I'm sure things have change."

"Not likely where we are headed."

They squinted at each other in silence.

"You must be packed and ready to go in forty-eight hours," Mac said then stood up. "Um, my condolences on your," he blurted then paused. "Your husband's untimely death."

Anya flashed Mac a surprised wide-eyed look. "Thank you, sir." She left the room confused by the sincerity of his last comment but sure about one thing. Commander Benson was an insufferable pompous ass.

TWELVE

A BLUSTERY WINTER'S wind caused Anya to stumble within steps of the Golden Gate Bridge. She wrapped her arms around the bronze urn and caught her balance. A back draft from a Greyhound bus flung her skirt into the air, exposing the backs of her legs. She could care less if her skirt flew up over her head, nothing would cause her to drop the jar.

She reached mid span and stopped to fill her lungs with sea air. On the horizon, iridescent sunlight pierced a thin layer of fog that reflected off several trawlers on their way to catch their daily haul of fish.

She propped the heavy container on the rail. Thoughts of Paval's betrayal meandered in and out of her mind. At one point, she wanted to dump the whole thing into a cesspool. But she reminded herself of the time she had tried to nurse a sick barn owl who screeched all night then died the next morning. Paval had wiped her tears and runny nose and comforted her in his arms for hours.

She held the jar to her lips and kissed it in honor of his memories.

Faced out to sea, she removed the lid then shut her eyes and said a silent prayer: *In sure and certain hope of the resurrection unto eternal life.*

She spilled his ashes over the edge. Fragments of dust swirled overhead then floated down into the water. She flung the empty urn towards the Far East.

"Return home, Paval, back to the arms of Mother Russia." She watched the ocean swallow his ashes. Her legs buckled and she gripped the railing faced with the realization that she was once again alone.

Anya walked through the rooms of her barren apartment. A Mission Street charity had picked up most of her furniture and kitchen items on Thursday. What remained, the girls would split amongst each other. Tomorrow she would be on a flight bound for China. The loud echo from her footsteps made her stomach flip flop. She had lived there for eight years, the longest she had ever lived anywhere. The remembrance of painting each room, decorating each room, cleaning each room, would never perish. But nothing held any significance other than a few of Paval's poems he had written for her.

She ran her hand along the arched entry to the living area and smiled. The only piece of furniture she would miss was a Duncan Phyfe chair that she had haggled over with a dealer then sold back to him for a profit.

Her hand rested on the knob of the front door as she took one last look. She preferred the emptiness to the collectible clutter from one's life. She turned and closed the door behind her.

Anya carried a small suitcase filled with a few articles of clothing as she entered Virginia's downstairs flat. Virginia insisted Anya stay at her place on her last night.

The apartment had a small living area with an eclectic décor. Against the wall, a faded flower-patterned blanket with threadbare edges covered a settee. A cardboard box substituted for a coffee table with several toys scattered about the hardwood floor.

"When are you going to pick up the coffee table I gave you? Anya said. "I also left you linens."

"I'll go over tomorrow." Virginia said. "How did your interview go with the Commander?" Her baby was propped on her hip and his hands clutched at her throat like a monkey. "Did he live up to your expectations?"

Anya crinkled her nose. "He's a troglodyte, arrogant and obstinate. Exactly what one would expect." She plopped on the davenport. "He doesn't want me to go. He thinks I'm a liability."

Virginia ignored Anya's complaint. "I saw him walking down the hall the other day. I think he's the handsomest man I've ever seen. He can't be more than thirty-five and so sheik, a real Clark Gable in his dress uniform." Virginia fluttered her eyelashes and laughed.

Anya frowned. "I need a drink. Maybe several."

"Help yourself, I'm going to put the baby to bed."

Virginia returned a few minutes later. "Anya, have you thought this over? Now that Paval . . . I mean, since the accident. Do you think it's wise to take this trip? You mentioned the Commander doesn't want you. Why go?"

Anya placed her drink on the makeshift coffee table. "I think it will do me more good to go, than to stay and pretend everything is normal. Besides, I have given my promise."

"I am sure under the circumstances, Mr. Atwater will understand if you reconsider."

Anya pulled on her finger and considered the

assignment. "I need this to heal my soul." She picked up her glass and took a sip.

Virginia said, "I'm not one to pry."

Anya rolled her eyes at Virginia.

"Okay, maybe I do," Virginia said.

"What is it you wish to ask?"

"Up till now, I've always been hesitant to ask. What's the story behind your finger twisting?" Virginia said.

Anya looked at her hand to see that she was rubbing her finger even while holding her glass. "I do it without thought." She let go of her finger.

"My papa returned to us from a summit with the Tsar on my sixteenth birthday. I'd raced out to greet him in an unladylike fashion. Mamma scolded me saying, I was now a woman and could no longer behave as a child. I pranced by her in defiance then ran upstairs to get ready for dinner."

Virginia chuckled, "You must have been a handful."

Anya shrugged. "Only child."

"At the dinner table, Papa talked about how fortunate we were to live in Vladivostok, away from the evil that stewed in a black caldron on the other side of the Urals. He remarked that Lenin and Trotsky inflamed the simple minds of the workers against the state. Gossip had become reality.

"Mamma put a quick stop to his rhetoric and

reminded him of the special day." Anya's voice lowered and she leaned towards Virginia, "Like I'd let him forget my birthday."

Virginia smiled.

"He remarked how grown up I'd become. I remember he looked at me with damp eyes then dabbed them with the corner of his napkin. I remember it so vividly because I don't recall him ever revealing that much emotion." Anya paused to reflect. She cleared her throat and continued.

"We retired to the parlor with cake. I knew he'd brought something wonderful from St. Petersburg. He never forgot to bring Mamma or me a gift upon his return travels. I forgot myself for a moment and bounced on the embroidered silk chaise in anticipation. I caught my mother's wrinkled brow and stopped red faced. For all her loving ways, Mamma became a tyrant when it came to propriety.

"Papa pulled a small black box from his inside coat pocket. He stated how much they both loved me. How proud they were I was their daughter. How I'd blossomed into a beautiful chamomile." Anya's arms went up in the air reminiscent of a dancing ballerina. "How my innocence represented the feathery white petals and my chaste body the lemon yellow center waiting to be pollinated."

Virginia's mouth curled into a sardonic twist.

Anya responded. "Every Russian thinks he's a poet."

"I remember him telling me I would marry soon and leave home." Anya shook her head and laughed. "I bristled, denounced marriage, and declared I would never leave my home."

"In the end," a deep sigh escaped her lips, "he was right."

"He handed me the box. My hands trembled with excitement. I flipped open the lid and found, nestled in black velvet, a luminous ring. The center stone cast a large purplish red hue that sparkled like a hall of mirrors. Small blue gems encircled the stone with white stones halfway down each side of the band. There lay the most exquisite object I'd ever seen. Karl Faberge had designed it especially for me.

"The stone, about the size of a dime, was a rare red diamond. It had been named the Kira after Mamma." Anya raised her shoulders. "For some reason they name large gems after people. They sent the diamond to the finest gem cutters in Amsterdam where they cut it into a unique octagon square shape called Asscher. The white, blue, and red colored gems symbolized the Russian flag.

"Papa drilled me as though I were a new recruit to remember proud Russian blood ran through my veins and to never walk in fear.

"That night, I promised I would never take the ring off and always stand unafraid to meet life's challenges head-on."

Anya looked at Virginia with wet eyes. "I did forget my promise and myself."

Virginia placed her arms around Anya. "Stay with me. We can look after each other."

Anya pulled away. "I've lived in a fog, similar to this city, afraid to face my past, afraid to commit to anything meaningful, afraid to take a chance on life. Shanghai is my last opportunity to reclaim myself. I have no choice but to return."

ANYA WOKE TO a sun filled morning after a fitful night. The sounds of giggles escaped from the other room. She dislodged herself from the cramped divan. Her back and legs felt relief as she stretched them out. She slipped on a floral robe and sauntered into the kitchen. Virginia, already dressed, held a spoon of Farina at her son's mouth. "Come on sweetie, open up for Mommy."

Anya poured herself a cup of coffee and pursed her lips at the thought of what today meant. She knew the hardest part of the day would be her farewell to Virginia.

"How did you sleep?" Virginia said.

"Fine." Anya lied. She sipped her coffee and watched Virginia feed her son. In some ways, she envied her. Virginia was at peace, knowing her husband was safe at a desk job rather than in the trenches. She had a healthy son to care for and love. A life Anya hoped one day she would possess but knew was impossible.

Virginia looked at Anya. "What?"

"Nothing. I should get dressed," Anya said. She placed her cup in the sink then retrieved her suitcase and went into the bathroom. After she finished dressing, she slipped the Wabun codebook Edmund Atwater had entrusted to her, into a brown leather satchel. She closed her eyes. She cleared her mind. She inhaled. "Okay, I'm ready."

Outside the bathroom door Virginia stood somber. Tears welled up in her eyes. Anya felt arms wrap tight around her shoulders.

"Virginia," Anya choked. "Let go. I can't breathe."

Virginia released her. "Sorry. I think I will miss you more than my husband." She wiped her eyes with her apron. "Come back safe."

"I don't know what the future holds, but I promise you that we will see each other again one day." Anya quelled her tears and headed for the door.

SHE ARRIVED AT Treasure Island's seaplane harbor. The docked Pan American Clipper made Anya's five-four frame seem minuscule. She stared at the aircraft's small propellers and wondered how this contraption would get airborne. She knew if she lingered for too long, she would never board.

Satchel in hand, she inhaled a breath of air then minced down the wooden walkway. Her heels reverberated which caused the other passengers and crew to turn. Head erect, shoulders back, she ignored their stares. Before she reached the airplane door, a loud clatter from the wooden planks caused her to look back. Macdonald Benson bounded down the boardwalk.

Anya dashed inside the plane. To her left she saw a spiral staircase. A uniformed woman guided her past the kitchen area and into a room with several fabric seats. Once seated, she buried her face in Daphne du Maurier's *Rebecca*, and hoped Mac would not sit next to her.

"Good day, Miss Pavlovitch. I hope you are comfortable," Mac said.

She pulled the book from her face with a clenched jaw. She tried to smile.

Mac turned and headed back down the aisle.

When the hostess came by to finalize takeoff, Anya looked around to see where Mac had gone. She spied him about two rows back. He had drawn his window curtain and thumbed through a magazine.

His eyes drifted up and locked with hers. He acknowledged her with a nod. Red-faced, she sat back in her seat. *Now why didn't he sit next to me?*

THIRTEEN
Pacific Ocean

TWO AIRCRAFT CARRIERS and thirty-eight hours later, Anya and Mac arrived on an island in the Pacific. A flock of gray gulls scattered as they taxied to a stop. Anya felt groggy from lack of a restful sleep. She lumbered down the airplane stairs to see a newly constructed airport tower that peered over a group of windblown coconut palms.

She and Mac climbed into a military chauffeur driven silver gray Ford sedan. She collapsed in the back seat. Without permission, she rested her head on Mac's shoulder and fell asleep.

Mac nudged her. "Wake up."

Anya yawned, stretched her arms, and sat up in her seat. Out the car window were rows of Quonset huts. At one end of the base was a hospital building with a painted red cross on the front. Military men dressed in kakis performed drills. Out the other side, she saw a large passenger ship along with several patrol boats scattered around an aquamarine lagoon.

The chauffeur turned around and said, "You'll be taken out to that liner."

Anya's stomach knotted up as though someone had punched her gut against her backbone. She swallowed hard and pushed thoughts of her last ocean voyage from her mind and prayed the sea would be merciful. She turned to Mac. "I didn't expect we'd travel on the ocean."

"We can't fly into China so this is our only alternative," he said. "The weather looks good, we should be all right."

A young man dressed in navy whites met them at the dock. They boarded a small metal dingy and motored over to the ship.

Mac climbed up the rope ladder first then leaned and held out his hand to Anya who stared at the ladder "Come on. You can do it," he said.

Anya placed one hand on the rope then the other. Her leg shook as she placed her foot onto the first rung and pushed herself up. She continued to climb while Mac reassured her. She reached the top and felt Mac grab her arms near the shoulders, then he hoisted her onto the deck.

"Thanks." She straightened her blouse and slacks and pushed her hair back into place.

Captain Olsen of the MS GRIPSHOLM welcomed them aboard. In a thick Scandinavian accent he said, "We're headed into rough seas for the next couple of days but according to the latest weather report, things should calm down before we reach Shanghai."

Anya groaned and rubbed her tummy.

"What's the matter," Mac whispered.

"I know you love the sea, but I don't."

Olsen said. "I'd be pleased if you would both be my guests for dinner."

"We'd be delighted," Mac said.

Anya rendered a polite smile, all the while, annoyed with Mac's perkiness.

Olsen motioned to the man next to him "My steward will escort you to your cabin. Let him know if you need anything."

"Cabin?" Anya leaned into Mac. "We're not married and I'm not sharing a room with you." His expression remained indifferent.

They climbed a flight of stairs to the main lobby. It had the appearance of a lavish hotel. A crystal chandelier hung from the center of a grand sweeping staircase. The polished white marble floor glistened from the reflective light above. It had been more than ten years since she crossed the ocean to America but that had been in bleak steerage.

Why in the world would they put us in the same cabin? Her palms turned clammy as they lumbered down a long corridor.

The Steward opened a compartment door. "This is your room, Madame. Let me know if you require anything. Dinner will be served at 8:30 PM. Commander Benson will be down the hall."

A wave of relief rushed over Anya when she entered. "Thank you, God," she said.

"Pardon?" the Steward said.

"I mean . . ." She turned towards Mac who wore a grin. Red faced she blurted, "I need a nap," then shut the door.

The pastel green colored cabin held a bed and two Queen Anne style chairs. A small round table between the chairs held a decanter of water with a tumbler glass turned upside down. Anya stood with her hands on her hips and laughed at her own foolishness.

THEY HAD BEEN at sea for several hours when the first signs of seasickness appeared. Flat on her back in bed, Anya massaged her belly. She glanced across at the porthole to the horizon. It appeared, then it was gone, then it appeared again. Up and down and up and down and up and down.

She failed to reach the toilet and spewed what

she had in her stomach onto the bathroom floor. Like a dog on her knees, she retched a few more times. She grabbed a towel to wipe her mouth and then held onto the sink to pull herself up. She threw the towel over the puke, fell onto the bed, and moaned into the pillow. "Ooooh, why did I agree to this?"

Moments later, she heard a knock at the door. A familiar voice said something through the door that she could not comprehend. She assumed it had to do with dinner, but food was not on her menu tonight.

AFTER DINNER, at Captain Olsen's invitation, Mac clambered up to the bridge. The storm had increased. A gust of wind ripped the bridge door from Mac's hand. An officer ran over to help as the rain pelted down on them both.

"Damn it, close that door," the Captain yelled.

"I guess the storm hit sooner than you expected," Mac said.

The Captain held a half smile. "We hold little influence over Mother Nature."

The control room held a maximum of four men. The large wheel and brass disc, where throttle commands bellowed down to the engine room, were reminiscent of Mac's experience during his tour of sea duty.

"Sorry I couldn't join you at dinner, but this storm has turned into a son-of-a-bitch," the Captain said. "How's the young lady?"

Mac shook off the sea spray. "I stopped by her cabin, but no answer. She must be asleep." He grinned, placed his hand on his stomach, and winked at the Captain.

A loud crash of water on the port side rolled the ship. They all staggered to regain their balance. "Straight into it, helmsman. What are you trying to do, sink us?" The captain turned to Mac. "This ship was built for trans-Atlantic travel. We deal with icebergs, not typhoons. Fortunately, this is only a gale." He flashed a smile.

"I've always preferred the pitch motion of a ship to calm waters. Unsettled seas give me peace," Mac said.

The captain ordered full speed ahead as the ship headed into a thirty-foot swell. Just as they reached the top, the wave broke and slammed down on the bow. A lifeboat broke loose and slammed against the rail. The ship continued up, then down the next swell.

Mac said, "It reminds me of the time I served aboard a destroyer. We'd just left Havana. God, what a paradise. Anyway, we got caught in a storm that spun into a major hurricane. We were up against forty-foot swells that almost sank us." He exaggerated as men tend do to impress one another. "It pulled off several hatches and flooded the bilge. We were fortunate to make it, though regrettably we lost a few good men."

"The sea is untamable, unyielding, and merciless," the Captain said.

Mac replied, "That she is and much more. But in her purest form, she is freedom."

The two men stared out the window of the bridge as the boat rocked and waves crashed on deck.

THE SEAS HAD calmed and the sun was at its strongest when Anya climbed topside. Her headache and queasiness had all but subsided. A salty breeze brushed her face as she walked through an open-air lounge. She imagined the pageantry of passengers who sat in wicker chairs with their tea and cakes and prattled on about current affairs.

She stepped onto the teak deck where once wealthy passengers lounged, now doctors, nurses, and missionaries sauntered. At the end of the promenade, a few played shuffleboard. Others wandered around in their own world. She wondered if they were thinking about the danger they were all sailing towards in Shanghai.

Dressed in a plain white blouse and tan slacks, she reclined in a deck chair. A pair of large dark sunglasses shielded her eyes. She raised her face to the sun and stretched. Seconds later, she heard Mac.

"How are your sea legs?" he said.

She gave him a quick look. "Better. The ashen tone in my face has gained some color."

"You've been barricaded in your cabin for so long I'd almost forgotten what you looked like."

She shrugged her shoulders. "Guess I'm a landlubber."

Mac's broad smile showed his perfectly formed white-ivory teeth. "I brought you something." He placed a bottle of Pepsi and sandwiches on the table next to her.

"Thanks." She gave him a curious glance. "I can't remember when I ate last." She sat up and took a nibble of sandwich then a sip of cola.

Mac sat on the chaise next to her and filled his pipe with tobacco. "We should be in Shanghai late tonight."

Anya let out a heavy sigh, slouched back, and bit her lower lip.

"That sounds ominous." Mac puffed on his pipe.

She inhaled the mild aroma with a hint of vanilla that filled the air. She was starting to enjoy the smell of a pipe. "I guess I have mixed emotions. It's been a long time since I've been in Shanghai." Anya wrenched down on her finger and tried to shake off an ominous feeling she had about their mission.

Mac's eyes widened. "I'm excited. I've never been to the Orient. I spent most of my career in Europe."

She studied him as he fiddled with his pipe. "What is it that you do Commander?"

He blinked. "Naval Intelligence."

"I understand the Navy. All boys dream of an ocean venture. But, what led you into intelligence?" she said.

He tilted his head forward and raised one eyebrow. "I was not what you'd call a model son, with an older sister and brother and one younger brother. I've always been somewhat of a troublemaker, so says my mother. Kid stuff mostly, like racing tractors, and not always ones that belonged to my family."

Anya looked over her sunglasses at Mac.

"I guess I should explain. I was brought up on a dairy farm in Maine." He laughed. "I remember one time a buddy and I had a bet as to who'd be the first to reach the top of this one hill. I was too young to hold a driver's license, but by law I could operate a tractor."

Anya held her smile. His expression was that of an excited boy telling a naughty tale.

"So there we both were, atop our tractors. We're neck 'n neck on a dirt road. My front wheel is just ahead of his. We're only a few feet from the top. And out of nowhere came old man Hamlen, barrel'n down on us in his shiny new Packard. Well, no one had time to stop. I swerved one way and my friend swerved the other and the old man passed between us. His car was fine, we both landed in ditches." Mac burst out laughing and slapped his knee, "They had to get another tractor to pull us both out."

Anya chuckled, "You're a bit of a wild hare aren't you? What did your papa say?"

"Well let's just say it was hard to sit for a few days." Mac drew in on his pipe and sat back in his chair.

"Gosh, my papa never laid a hand on me. In fact, I don't remember it being anything he'd consider."

"Different cultures I guess. I know your father was a military man. What did he do?"

"He was a great man," she said. "A Chevalier Guard. Once considered a very elite group of men, he protected the Tsar and Tsarina. My grandpapa saved Tsar Alexander II's life from an assassination attempt. After that, my family became a favorite with the Romanovs." Anya tugged on her finger.

"Your finger, does it hurt?" Mac said.

Anya pursed her lips. "It's a habit. Similar to the way you fiddle with your pipe.

Mac looked at his pipe and smiled.

Her attention wandered to a young man and woman as they approached. Anya saw their hands brush against each other. The woman's cheeks blushed and she bowed her head. The man cast a smile her way as they passed. Anya wondered what secrets they shared. She hoped blissful, unlike her own. She felt a tinge of jealousy and thought of Paval. *It seems decades since I last saw him, yet it's been less than a week.* A pang of guilt swept over her. It just occurred to her that she had blindsided him with the news of her leaving, which may have led to his death.

Mac stirred in his seat.

"You were explaining how you got into Naval Intelligence," she said.

"I went to college in New Hampshire. I wanted to get away from the farm, but not too far, in case my folks needed me. The area is agrarian, not a great place for kids filled with a lot of juice." He paused then scratched his chin. "To add to our excitement a pal and I decided we'd run up to Canada and get some hooch . . . liquor, you know."

Anya nodded.

"We'd sneak up there on an isolated dirt road, bring back the stuff, and sell it to fellow students." He guffawed. "We were hauling in the money until one night we ran into the law on the way back into the states. It was during prohibition, therefore a serious offense."

"Did you go to prison?" she said.

"Nah, my Uncle got me out of any prison time under the promise to the courts that I'd enlist in the military. I chose the Navy because I didn't want to get shot and die in a trench in France, like my eldest brother." Mac stared out in the distance.

"I must have done right." He shrugged. "After a stint, the Navy sent me to the War College in Rhode Island."

"Did you prefer that college?" Anya said.

His demeanor seemed uplifted and his eyes cast a twinkle. "Loved it."

"We studied strategic and tactical problems. How to gather social, political, economic, industrial information then analyze and report conditions. Because I'm fluent in German, the Department of Naval Intelligence recruited me right away. They gave me a German passport and told me to wander around Germany."

"A spy?" she said.

"Not really. It was in between the two wars. I scouted the Nazi party. I worked with them, yet worked against them and they hadn't a clue," he paused. "I guess it was Intelligence."

"Have you ever—killed someone?" she said.

"I had to strangle a woman once."

"God," she said. "You seem so—so dispassionate."

"It was a long time ago," he said.

She remembered the phone conversation he had with a woman named Helen. "Who is Helen?" she said.

He gave her a solemn look. "My wife. I also have a young daughter. They are currently with her folks." His shoulders slumped and he began to fidget with his pipe.

A steward with a boyish grin approached and asked if they required any further refreshments. They both politely said no. He removed their plates when one dropped to the ground and shattered. A trace of cherry red swept his cheeks. Heads turned. His face now scarlet, he scurried to pick up the pieces then scuttled away.

"Poor boy," she said.

"He was looking at you and not paying attention," he said.

"How do you know he wasn't looking at you," she said.

Mac laughed. "What about your upbringing?"

"I thought you'd already uncovered everything

about me." She flipped a lock of her hair behind one shoulder.

"The file I was given only accounted for the years once you arrived in America."

"What is it that you want to know?"

"How did you come to America?"

"Well, you know about my papa."

Mac nodded and chewed on his pipe. Anya watched the gentle breeze carry the smoke away.

She directed a glance his way. "After many years of the Tsar handing over money to greedy relatives, my papa became disillusioned and requested a transfer to Vladivostok. It's on the Sea of Japan, where the Trans-Siberian Railway ends. We lived there for many years. That's where I learned to speak Chinese and Japanese. Its diverse culture pulled me in. I couldn't learn enough about them."

"Why did you leave Russia?" Mac said.

"When the Bolsheviks murdered the Tsar and his family . . ." She softened her voice. "I remember the Romanov girls. I grew up with them. They were beautiful, delightful young women. I blame that cold-blooded English Monarchy. They had an opportunity to rescue them but failed. I don't understand how someone could abandon their own relations. Bastards."

Mac squirmed in his seat. She wondered if he was thinking of his family.

She continued. "My papa put my mamma and me on a ship to Shanghai then he joined the White Army against the Reds. "I was almost seventeen when I arrived in Shanghai." She chuckled and tossed her head back. "China is a strange land. It's nothing like any other place in this world. We were fish out of water as the saying goes.

"At the time, the Chinese were fearful from the onslaught of refugees that poured into their country. They worried they'd lose their identity. Many shunned us and a few even threw stones at us. It was a struggle for my mamma and me.

"Less than a year later, the White Army had been crushed and my papa returned to us. His arrival provided a more comfortable life." Anya recalled Paval's letter admitting he had betrayed her father. She rose from her chair to stretch and took a deep breath of ocean air.

Mac relit his pipe. "What did your father do in China?" Smoke billowed from his lips.

Anya returned to her seat. "He wrote for a Russian newspaper owned by a Chinese family before his disappearance."

"Disappearance? I read that both your parents died."

Anya lay back in her chair and placed one arm across her forehead. "It was my eighteenth birthday, truly, my last happy day. My best friend

Bia, her baba or father owned the newspaper where my papa worked. She and I were to meet my parents at the Cathay Hotel. A place where, on occasion, you'd find diplomats, opium dealers, and international spies mingling together." Anya tilted her chin up. "Very chichi."

"I was anxious to see my mother. In my haste, I'd forgotten my ring on the dresser and she'd called and promised to bring it. I'd spent most of the day at Bia's preparing for my party. We laid out our gowns, hats, and long white gloves. We believed we were very grown up. By late afternoon, everything unraveled. A major earthquake hit the southern region. It demolished several villages and caused severe damage throughout the city.

"I ran without thought anxious to get home to my parents." She rubbed her finger. "I remember racing through the streets. I can still hear the children's screams and the wails of men and women. Broken glass and debris were scattered everywhere. I remember the crackle of broken wires danced about reminiscent of fireworks. Fallen bodies from exposed buildings littered the streets. It resembled a bombed-out city." She wiped her tears on her blouse sleeve.

"I made my way home only to find that my parents weren't there. I assumed they were out searching for me, so I went to the hotel. They weren't there either, and no one remembered seeing them. I went back to the house. Morning came, and they hadn't returned.

"I searched every hospital and morgue for months, but I never found a trace of either. Officials told me they were probably in one of the mass graves used to bury the hundreds who had died that day. In some way, I still hope to find them."

"I'm sorry for your loss," Mac said. "I remember when we received the news of my brother's death." He gave her an inquisitive look. "How did you survive?"

Anya twisted her lips and chewed the inside of her cheek. *Even though he has shown kindness, I still don't trust him. I won't. I can't. I shouldn't go on.* But the words spilled out.

"When you're young you can cope with just about anything if your parents are there to help, such as the loss of a family pet, a close friend, relocating to a unfamiliar land with odd customs, but when you lose both parents something at a very primal level gets twisted up inside."

Anya cleared her throat and fidgeted with a button on her blouse. "Some people just shut down emotionally and die. However, the lucky ones . . . the very lucky ones have a sense of self-preservation that takes hold in unimaginable ways.

You're alone, cold and hungry with the realization that no one will come to rescue you. It sets off alarms. You can't afford to think about right or wrong, the future or past. It's only the present that concerns you. You don't realize the choices you make will affect the person you'll become."

Anya brought her knees to her chest, embraced her legs, and looked past the ship's railing. "I don't know if this information is in my file but I was born to aristocracy with wealth and all its privileges."

Mac nodded.

"I fully expected to take my place in Russian society next to the royal family. I'd have married a military man, as had my mamma and her mamma and her mamma before her. My life would have included galas, children, and endless summers at the Black Sea. I'd have been fulfilled in that role, subservient to my husband.

"It's not until you're confronted with your own mortality that you find yourself doing the unexpected." She stared into Mac's blue eyes.

"I never imagined that I'd become a courtesan, and certainly not one in Shanghai."

His straight-faced appearance didn't surprise her. She guessed his training would not allow him to react. He did, however shift slightly in his chair.

"You don't just wake up one day and say, um . . . I'll go have sex and acquire some money.

Prostitution creeps up on you, similar to falling asleep." She stroked one cheek against her knees. "One night you go to a cabaret flooded with American sailors. You just want to laugh and have some harmless fun. At some point, someone whispers in your ear and tells you how beautiful you are, and how much he loves you. You start to believe those whispers, because it sustains you."

Mac gripped his pipe with his teeth and puffed.

"Seduction is hypnotic. Oddly enough, after my parents' disappearance, I found that being close with someone, albeit a stranger comforted me." She reclined in her seat. "I felt desperate for someone's affection. I met a man who promised to take care of me. He made me feel safe. I ate regular meals again and had somewhere to sleep." A smile crossed her lips. "His name was Pete, a good man and so handsome in his naval uniform."

Mac's eyebrows rose.

"The U.S. Navy came to Shanghai to protect American business interests. Pete was a gunner on a patrol boat on the Yangtze River. We were so happy together." She felt light-headed and took a sip of soda. "Then one day the devil knocked at my door and told me I was too happy. Ambushed by bandits is what they said. I'm standing at the door six months pregnant. Pete is dead and I'm alone again."

Mac offered her his handkerchief.

"I lost the baby a few days later." Anya dabbed her eyes and blew her nose. "The doctors said I'd never be able to have more children. I was a real mess after that." She handed the hankie back to him.

"Keep it," he said.

"Pete's buddies saw I needed help, so they forged wedding documents that allowed me to travel to America. Oh, I suppose I shouldn't have told you that. Don't tell anybody."

"It was a long time ago," he said.

"Anyway, they got me on a ship to San Francisco. I will always be grateful to those sailors because without them I know I wouldn't be alive today."

She sipped her soda pop. "Things happen to people when they get broken and they can't always put themselves back together the way they'd like. You make impetuous decisions when you think there's no hope for a future. It's a funny thing to let go of dreams. It's living, but not really."

She shifted herself to an upright position and wiped her brow. "I don't regret any choices I made. I did what I had to do to stay alive."

"We all carry a bit of hell with us like a turtle in his shell," Mac said.

She stood up and sighed, "I'm tired now. I

think I'll get some rest. She took a few steps then stopped and turned around. "Funny thing—it's kind of liberating spilling your entrails to a stranger."

MAC'S EYES FOLLOWED Anya as she sauntered away. The sunlight shimmered across her Titian red hair as the wind carried strands into the air. She walked with a confidence that he had not seen in American women. Her head erect, her shoulders back, gave her an arched look, and her stride gave the impression she walked a tight rope. He appreciated her form and elegance. But he also knew she held an unpredictable iron will that spelled trouble with a capital T.

Her ability to speak freely about such intimate details made him uncomfortable. There were moments during her cathartic confession when he wanted to walk away. He had gained an appreciation for what she lived through. He admired, almost envied, her relationship with her parents. His own parents had married to combine farms. They were stern, demanding, and distant with their affection. Hard work became the family mantra, anything less was deemed devil's play.

His eyes narrowed. *Wait a minute.* Blood rushed to his cheeks. *Did she just try to manipulate me?* He turned his head towards the way she had left, but she had vanished. *If she'd been hankering for sympathy, she served her dish to the wrong person. No one can control people better than me, especially when it comes to women.*

FOURTEEN
Shanghai

T HE WATERS WERE calm when they entered the mouth of the Whangpoo River. Mac stood at the bow and saw a glow of lights through a thick mist. They would soon be in Shanghai and there life would not be tranquil.

Motoring along the river, he saw cannons strategically positioned in their direction. This was his first indication they had entered enemy territory. Thoughts of his family emerged. He remembered his wife and daughter built a snowman on his last day. He had not joined them but rather watched from their living room window. Mac fought to erase their images and vowed never to think of them again.

Anya approached and stood next to Mac. Together they watched in silence as the city lights drew nearer. Moments later, several other passengers made their way on deck.

"What can you tell me about Shanghai?" Mac said.

She crinkled her nose. "Moments away from arriving in port and you pick this time to inquire about this oriental gem."

"Seems as good a time as any," he said.

"I couldn't possibly tell you everything in a single conversation. What I can say is that it's a very old city shrouded in mystic lore and ancient tradition. It's tightly controlled by unscrupulous people who are vigilant to hold on to their kernel of power."

"You mean the drug lords?" Mac said.

"I mean them as well as the many foreign nations who have a vital stake in the city."

"Come now, Miss Pavlovitch, you can't mean that we Americans and the British are gangsters?"

She directed her comment towards Shanghai. "I know there's great wealth in this city and those in control ensure things don't change."

The smell of petrol and oil permeated the cold air. They cruised along the city's shoreline. Tall structures gave the cityscape a modern day presence. Lights illuminated the area with a glow like a halo. The juxtaposition of sampans, rickshaws and neoclassical buildings presented a mixture of old and new. "I feel like I could be in a European or American city," he said.

"Shanghai is known as the Paris of the East," Anya said. "This area is called The Bund. It's the financial center of this province."

"What happened here?" Mac pointed to the crumbled buildings and monuments.

Her smile withered. "This must be the aftermath from the Japanese bombs in '37. I'd left for America by then. There is a fierce hatred between these two nations that goes back hundreds of years." A long wistful sigh passed her lips. "It was magnificent in its day. If you had money the city was yours to rule."

The ship docked as white-clad Japanese soldiers positioned themselves along the pier. Everyone on board watched an envoy of armed forces board. One of the soldiers spoke to Captain Olsen for several minutes before the militia departed.

Shipboard whispers ran wild as Anya and Mac made their way down to the Captain.

"The Japanese have posted sentries with orders not to let anyone off," Olsen said. "No medical personnel, missionaries and especially no Red Cross can disembark." He scratched his head, which caused his cap to tilt to the side. "Commander Benson, I don't know how you'll get to dry land."

Mac glanced at the gangplank that remained attached. "We'll need a diversion, something to take them away from their posts. Any thoughts?" He gave Anya a hawkish stare.

The hairs on the back of her neck stood straight up. She knew she was in it now, with no way out.

"I see from the look on your face you have something to say," Mac said.

"I'm concerned," she paused. "We don't have a plan. My father used to say, a man without a plan ignores the simple signs of danger. This is where mistakes are encountered, and lives are lost unnecessarily."

"Have a little faith would you?" he said.

Oh why did I agree to return after all these years? In her heart, she knew the answer.

"I have an idea," the Captain rubbed his hands together. "Don't worry you two. Position yourselves near the gangplank and get ready to go when you see the signal." He ran down to join a group of doctors.

"Signal?" Anya turned to Mac. "What do you think they plan to do?"

"Not sure, but it better be dramatic to move the guards to the far side of the dock. We can slip passed them when their backs are to us."

Anya and Mac crouched near their exit and watched a doctor soak an overstuffed chair with liquid.

Mac said, "It must be diesel fuel."

"What are they going to do—burn the ship to get us off?" Anya said.

"No. Watch. This is brilliant."

Several doctors hoisted up the chair while another flung a lit match, and hurled it overboard. It hit the ground with a loud crash followed by an enormous explosion with flames that soared twenty feet up into the sky.

The sentries dashed over to investigate and Mac yelled at Anya "Head for those crates." They rushed down the ship's plank and ran towards a tall stack of crates several yards ahead. They stopped when they reached the crates. Hidden, Anya felt her heart race and tried to take short breaths. Mac peered around the side of the stack. The fire was starting to die down and one sentry had gone back to his post. They still had several feet before they would be out the enemies' sight.

Mac moved to the other side of the crate and looked up at the ship. The Captain nodded to Mac then yelled down at the soldiers. It caused the guards heads to turn away. At that moment, Mac grabbed Anya by the hand and they stole into the darkness.

Once safely away, Mac stopped, bent over and laughed "Did . . . you . . . see that chair?" He caught his breath. "The sight of those doctors tossing it over was too much."

Anya's chuckle turned into hysterical laughter. Streams of tears trickled down her cheeks. She covered her mouth to stifle the panic that swelled within. A combination of exhaustion and fear had taken hold of her.

Mac placed his arm around her and drew her close. "We're okay." He patted her back. "You were quite a trooper. The worst of it is over."

Anya suspected his words were hollow. She regained her composure and wiped the last of her tears from her face, then inhaled. "I'm all right, momentary lapse," She shook her head. "It won't happen again."

"Which way to the American Consulate?" Mac said.

She gave him a mock salute and motioned him to follow. Anya led Mac down a labyrinth of passageways selecting the darkest path. On several occasions, she had to backtrack because she had lost her way. She halted in her tracks, which caused Mac to bump into her.

"I hear voices," she whispered. They both froze. She felt his hot breath on the back of her neck.

Mac stretched his arm across Anya's collarbone and forced her against the brick building. In silence, they waited as two soldiers passed within several feet of them. Once the soldiers were out of sight, she threw his arm off her.

"Don't do that again," she said. "I know what it means to hide. You're not my Chevalier Guard."

"Look," he said. "I don't know you and you don't know me, but we're in this together. I need to make sure that nothing happens to derail this assignment. If that means a little discomfort on your part—too damn bad." He marched a few steps.

"You're headed in the wrong direction," she said then muttered under her breath, "Jackass."

THEY SAW A Japanese sentry lurking about in the shadows as they approached the American Consulate. A dim streetlight and myriad of leafless trees blocked a full view of the building.

"Now what?" Mac said.

"You didn't expect we were going to waltz in through the front door?"

"How do we get in?"

"Hang on, I need to orient myself," Anya replied in a low voice. She closed her eyes to regain faded memories. "American Consulate on the right and the Dutch Consulate down the street and to the left."

"What are you mumbling?" he said.

She put her finger to her lips. "Shush, I can't

remember where the entrance is."

"The entrance to what?" Mac said. "The consulate front door is directly ahead."

"I know you can't see me that well in the dark, just know that I'm rolling my eyes at you. Come on—this way."

They slipped down a darkened alley then to a narrow street. She stopped and pointed to a manhole cover. "See if you can lift this." Mac obeyed. After a couple of guttural grunts he pushed the heavy metal lid aside.

Anya climbed down the iron ladder first.

Mac said, "I guess you've overcome your fear of ladders."

"I've decided to pretend I'm a character in a Nero Wolf novel. Besides I like being in control. It makes this situation tolerable."

A pungent stench of human waste wafted upward when Anya reached the bottom that made her choke. She felt moisture and heard water slosh beneath her feet. The only light source available came from the streetlight above. She felt her way along the cold moist stony wall in search of something.

Mac descended the ladder. His frame did not allow him to stand up straight. "What is this place?"

"How it was explained to me," Anya continued to feel her way along the wall. "Shanghai is relatively flat and vulnerable to high tides. Years ago, the British wanted to protect their investment so they built an immense network of underground tunnels to control the rising tides.

"How do you know about this place?" he said.

"Certain high profile people needed to keep their private lives well hidden, so when they wished to go somewhere unseemly or have a clandestine rendezvous they used this corridor. They nicknamed it the *Underground* after the London subway."

"That's not what I asked," Mac said.

She ignored his persistence. "Found it." She removed the lantern from its hiding spot. Give me your matches," she ordered.

"My what?"

"Matches. You must have matches in one of those pockets."

He handed them over then jumped and hit his head. "What the hell. Something ran across my foot."

Anya chuckled. "Rats. There are hundreds of them down here."

"I hate rats."

"I find it amusing that a man trained to endure torture fears a few rats. I think two-legged species are more dangerous," she said.

"I've seen a rat walk on his hind legs," Mac said.

"Please let there be oil in this contraption." She struck off a spark that ignited the lamp. The light illuminated a tunnel that seemed to go on forever.

"Let's pray the Japanese are more occupied with the security of shipping lanes, roadways, and train stations, and haven't bothered to search under their feet," Mac said.

"I guess we'll find out soon enough," Anya replied.

They continued their trek, taking left and right turns until they arrived at a narrow passageway. At the end of the corridor was a large stone wall. It appeared impenetrable. She groped for a particular spot then gave a slight shove to the left side of the massive stone. It gave way.

"Glad you came along for the ride," Mac said.

"I reserve the right to agree when we're back home."

They passed under the threshold of a small door where Anya found herself on a white marble floor that sparkled from chandelier light. Two symmetrical barrels from a tarnished shotgun stared her in the face.

Mac emerged and stepped in front of Anya.

"Whadda we have here?" the voice carried a heavy American southern drawl.

The gun holder was a Caucasian man, medium height, middle-aged, with a round button nose and ruddy complexion. He wore an ivory tunic top and pants. Next to him, stood a slender Chinese man who looked about twenty. He sported oversized black round-rimmed spectacles. His hairstyle was reminiscent of an American lad parted down the side and trimmed around his ears. He wore a red sweater over a white collared shirt with slacks that appeared a size too big. A thin-lipped smile crossed his face.

Anya thought it strange that the Westerner was dressed in Chinese attire and the Chinese in American fashion.

"I am Commander Macdonald Benson." Mac exposed the palms of his hands. "I'm going to reach into my pocket." He withdrew a document from inside his jacket.

The man's cheeks bulged into a broad grin as he read the note. "Sorry for the rude reception." He lowered the gun. "Ya just don't know who to expect through that door these days. I am the American Attaché here in Shanghai. Sheldon Beaumont. Call me Shelley and this here is Joe. My valet, boy Friday, you name it. I couldn't live without him." Shelley laid his hand on Joe's shoulder. Anya observed Shelley's hand rested longer than considered polite.

Anya yawned. "Excuse me," she said. "It's just that I am simply exhausted."

"Child, let's get y'all out of those wretched clothes and into a hot bath," Shelley said.

Anya felt the pressure of a fingertip touch her back as he nudged her up the stairs.

"The food supply is somewhat limited as ya can imagine," he said. "I'll have our cook whip you up a light meal and deliver it to all y'all's room. Most of the staff has been evacuated and what remains will leave with the ship y'all came in on."

"You're not leaving on the ship?" Mac said.

Shelley smiled. "We have converted much of our upper floor into bedrooms to accommodate unexpected guests who have revolved in and out of here since the war." He opened the bedroom door and motioned Anya to enter. "I think ya be comfortable in here, darlin. Good night and have a pleasant rest."

Anya surveyed the powder blue bedroom with its white French provincial decor. The center of the room held a massive bed with curved lines and quintessential shell motif on the head and footboard. An elaborate scalloped mirror hung on the opposite side. Below it, sat an exquisitely carved dressing table. She imagined perfumes, powders, and jewels draped across the tabletop. On the other side of the room stood a huge armoire. Inside, the smell of cedar lingered among shoes and gowns. Most likely from a former resident, she thought.

The raw sewage odor that drifted up from her body prompted her to head to the bathroom that was adjacent to her room. She caught her reflection in the mirror and screamed, "Oh God." Her hair had frizzed into the shape of a large beach ball and black sludge streaked her face.

The steamy water from the bathtub penetrated her aching muscles. She rested her head against the white porcelain tub and sunk until her chin reached water level. Her skin prickled as the bath salts caressed her body. She melted into the contour of the tub and contemplated how she would make contact with her old friend Bia.

FIFTEEN

S HELLEY DIPPED A piece of fried bread into his bowl of rice congee and scooped out the last drops. He swallowed and smacked his lips. "It's a good bet them Japs 'ill soon collect all enemy civilians for internment." He pushed the empty bowl away. "The ship you came in on may be the last of its kind allowed in these here waters."

Mac put his hands behind his head and interlocked his fingers. "It's a more serious situation than I'd been led to believe."

Shelley displaced a toothy grin. "Bill Donavan—he never quite tells anyone the whole truth and expects y'all assume a lot. Some folks in the States think Bill is running an American Gestapo. For me, well—he's a stubborn hot-headed Mik, but he loves his country."

Shelley leaned back from the desk and scratched

his head. "I spect things 'ill get worse around here. It's an odd situation between the Limeys and the Japs. A test of wills, ya might say. Both are arrogant sons of bitches who believe they're the superior race. But the Japs have one up on the Brits—they control Shanghai."

Shelley went to the credenza, poured himself a cup of tea. "We've found out the hard way that the Jap military is not a very humane sovereignty. The worst of 'em are the Kempeitai, a Jap police force."

He returned to his seat. "Have ya heard of 'em?"

"I understand that they specialize in interrogation methods," Mac said.

"Those who fall prey to their torture techniques don't usually survive." Shelley glanced at Mac. "I'm told a prominent editor of the China Press was brought aboard the GRIPSHOLM this morning. His feet were solid black. God knows what those devils did to him. Most likely, they'll need to amputate 'em both, poor bugger." He sipped his tea. "You can see what you're up against."

Mac's muscles stiffened. When he had agreed to take on this assignment, the risk did not appear so grave. He questioned the reason then reminded himself of the Navy's motto, *not self but country.*

"By the way, what's y'all's cover?"

"I believe that task has been left to you," Mac said.

Shelley hooted, "That Bill."

"And I'll need an introduction to a U sang, U sing."

"Du Yu-seng." Shelley sat up. "Do ya know about him?"

Mac shook his head.

"Yu-seng funds Chiang Kai-shek's nationalist government and in return, he controls drug-deals and labor unions. He's basically a gangster who calls himself a public welfare worker. The chap I was telling you about with the feet, we think Yu-seng's people handed him over to the Japs for printing negative comments about him." Shelley opened the right desk drawer. "The Japs think Yu-seng is in Chungking but I know he's here in Shanghai, hiding out." Shelley snickered. "You know these high profile gangsters have to stay on the move."

"Do y'all speak French?" Shelley said.

Mac hesitated. "Je parle un petit peu de français."

"Excellent." Shelley rifled through some papers in a drawer and pulled out a folder. "Let's introduce ya as Monsieur Rene Barnaud, a French exporter."

"Exporter of what?" said Mac.

"Opium, my dear boy. Opium is the linchpin of

Shanghai and Yu-seng keeps the wheel turning."

"Why French?"

"For one thing Yu-seng speaks French, and for another, the French are the least harassed people in Shanghai. The Vichy government is in cahoots with the Japs," Shelley sneered. "But there are a few pseudo Vichy French who work with a small Gaullist resistance group here. Most of the allied communities can be trusted. Many of 'em work in one way or another with the OSS." Shelley continued to rifle through the drawer.

Mac caught sight of Joe from the corner of his eye enter the room with the stealth of a cat. He wondered where he learned that trick. Mac acknowledged him. "Good morning, Joe." He studied the boy. "Why do they call you Joe?"

Still rummaging through papers, Shelley stopped and looked up. "Because he's always got his nose in one of those crazy Hardy Boys books. The main character's name is Joe. He even dresses like him, down to the red sweater and slacks.

Joe said, "They're swell reading and I learn how to speak American."

Mac laughed. "My younger brother read those books when he was a kid."

Shelley cleared his throat. "The Commander needs to go to the Market."

"Yu-seng's place?" Joe backed up.

"Yeah." Shelley handed Mac a sealed envelope. "This should get you in to see Yu-seng. We can get you additional identification papers when you return."

Mac spotted Shelley's glance in Joe's direction and speculated on what it meant.

THE LATE MORNING sun peeked through the curtains and roused Anya from her bed. Mac had already gone; she had heard him wander around his room at daybreak. It had been too early and too cold for her to venture out from under the warm covers.

She walked over to the armoire and opened the door. She shrieked as a tiny gray mouse scurried past her. She slapped her hand to her lips and laughed at herself. *You've got greater issues at hand than a harmless rodent.*

Inside, she found her tan slacks and white blouse laundered. At the bottom of the wardrobe lay her shoes, cleaned and polished. Her stomach rumbled as she dressed.

Anya headed down to breakfast. She passed by Shelley's office to find him writing.

"I trust y'all slept well," Shelley said.

She entered the room. Shelley folded a piece of paper in half as she neared the desk. "Very well, thank you. Is Mr. Benson around?"

"Oh no my dear, he and Joe went out some time ago." Shelley placed the letter in the drawer and rose from his chair. "The Commander would like ya to sit tight till he returns."

"I thought I'd walk around the city. I'll be back before Mac realizes I'm gone. I promise."

Shelley hesitated and pulled on one earlobe. "You'd best be back quick or he'll be madder than a box of frogs."

Anya giggled at his southern colloquialism.

"Before y'all can go out we'll need to get ya some papers." His face took on a morbid expression. "All Occidentals must register with them Japs and are forced to wear armbands so they can ID us without looking at our papers. You must use extreme caution when outside this compound."

"I understand the gravity."

"Ah sugar, I assume you speak French?" Shelley said.

"*Oui*," Anya replied.

"Excellent. We're all Frenchmen today."

"Excuse me?" Anya cocked her head to one side.

"I have established Commander Benson as a French businessman. He slapped his hands together. "Okay then child, let's go fix you some vittles."

ANYA PUSHED HER rice and vegetables around the plate at the kitchen table. "Your accent, I don't recognize it. Are you from New England?"

Shelley choked on a sip of tea and snorted, "Lord, no child. I'm no Yankee. I'm a yellowhammer from the heart of Dixie. God's country, Alabama." He continued to chuckle.

Anya's face flushed and she lowered her head.

"Sorry for the outburst but I haven't had a good laugh like that in years."

Anya grinned.

"My family farms cotton. Have since the days of slavery. Now mostly they use prisoners. Cheapest labor money can buy."

"How did you end up here?" she said.

"I made up my mind at a very young age that I didn't want to plow, pick, or produce cotton. In college, I got interested in politics. Didn't care too much for the affairs of the state a little too narrow-minded if ya figure what I mean." He winked. "I funded a national campaign and in return received appointments abroad. Been here pert near fifteen years. I've lived in Australia, the Philippines, Siam, and even some time in Japan but China is my home. I plan to die here, hopefully not for some time, and have my ashes thrown into the Yangtze."

Shelley sipped on his tea while Anya finished eating. "Sugar, you best be careful and keep a low profile. Avoid major streets. Soldiers march up and down to intimidate the Shanghailanders." Shelley gave her a stern glance. "Seeking old friends could prove dangerous. Y'all don't know where one's loyalties lie these days."

Anya's heart thumped two beats too fast. *How'd he know what I was contemplating?* She listened to his warning but knew that Bia would never betray her. Their friendship had endured too much. After her parents' disappearance, they drifted apart. Anya had associated herself with other Russian women in the same situation, alone and desperate for money. She had cut ties with Bia to gain entry into the social clubs where she made her living. Having close ties with a Chinese family invited exclusion within the European community. Shame washed over her.

Shelley handed Anya her papers. "You can leave through the front door. The new sentry won't know when you came in. They ain't that rigid regarding the coming and going of people. It's probably because they want to see who comes a calling."

She thanked him for the papers and left. At the sentry post, she hoped her trembling hand would not give her away as she presented her papers. The sentry scrutinized them, gave her a look of disgust and motioned her to move ahead.

She took a deep breath and headed to the one

place in Shanghai she knew would receive her with open arms.

SIXTEEN

B ENT OVER, Mac followed Joe, who held a torch, down into the underground tunnel. They headed in a different direction than he and Anya had taken the night before. The same mildewed smell filled his nostrils.

"Didn't Shelley pay off the guards so we wouldn't have to use this passageway?" Mac said.

"Yeah, but this quick. Safe for you," Joe replied.

"Why is the tunnel dry? Last night Anya and I walked through some kind of black sludge that covered the ground."

"You and Miss Anya entered farther south by sea level. Lots of flooding that way. We go higher, away from sea."

"It still smells like crap," Mac said.

Rats squealed and scuttled through the tunnel. It brought back his memory as a small child when his older brother, as a prank, locked him in a rat-infested shed.

After what seemed to Mac an eternity, they made their way out of the tunnel through a wooden door. Light beamed down from a colorful leaded glass ceiling. Mac inhaled delightful aromatic scents of licorice and jasmine. "Ah, what are these wonderful smells?" He glanced around the room and spotted hundreds of stacked glass jars filled with what looked like dried twigs and weeds. "What is this junk?"

"Junk," Joe said. "Maybe to western eyes. These priceless herbs. It's uncle's tea shop. He famous throughout China."

"What the hell are these?" Mac pointed to containers that held dried lizards stacked side-by-side, black beetles with stiffened legs, and other dried insects.

"Uncle also medicine man. Insects treat colds to cancer." He picked up a clear glass bottle. "This centipede relieve headache and heal snakebite."

"That's nice." Mac hurried his pace out the shop's front door. Outside, he came to an abrupt stop. The scene before him was unlike the European port section of Shanghai they passed while aboard ship.

The sky was streaked with a myriad of electrical wires that zigzagged from one dilapidated building to the next. Short tomato red sashes with cryptic markings hung along the wires and fluttered in the breeze. Small light bulbs used to illuminate the street at night alternated between the sashes. Car horns blasted and shouts boomed. Hordes of Chinese scurried around by foot or rickshaw or bicycle in black wide-legged pants and soiled white tunic tops. Open-air shops displayed apple green jade stones, white statues of Buddha and hand-painted scrolls that depicted bamboo trees with exotic birds in flight.

"Where are we?" Mac said.

"You in ancient walled city. Wall destroyed long ago but invisible barrier preserves our culture."

Joe picked up a stick and drew an X in the dirt street. "Here we are. North lies International Settlement, where we come from. West is French Concession, probably Miss Anya once live. The Bund, you saw last night, runs north along the river. Farther north, other side of smelly river. No go there," Joe waved at Mac. "Many Japanese. They lock up Jews, Communists, writers, anyone they no like."

Mac remembered what Shelley had told him earlier, about the reporter's blackened feet from torture.

Numerous almond-eyed people glared at Mac as they passed by. A few sneered and grunted, others ignored him. An elderly prune-faced woman shuffled by and spat on his shoes. Joe tried to intervene but Mac held him back. "To them I'm just another invader."

Mac's mouth gaped open at the commerce that thrived in the midst of foreign occupation. "How do these merchants continue to prosper under Japanese scrutiny?" he said.

Joe jammed his hands on his hips and puffed out his chest. "Shanghailanders are smooth talker. They sell you anything. Everything have a price." Joe rubbed the tips of his thumb and index finger together.

"Centuries we under one thumb or another, yet no one put stranglehold on us. You see—even though they think we vain, we Shanghailanders are most innovative."

Two Chinese men on the other side of the street yelled at each other. Mac opened his stance and lifted his hands in preparation for a blow across the chin.

"No worry Mac, it's cool, street brawls okay. They filled with wild hand waves and big talk but no real blows." Joe laughed as he watched the two men exchange words.

Mac loosened up his shoulders. "I admire your cultural pride, even when your people are at each other's throats."

Ahead, a rusted out navy blue motorcar powered by a dapple-gray horse ambled down the road. A carriage replaced the car's chassis. An elderly man sat slumped over and looked more fatigued than the horse that pulled the buggy. "It taxi," Joe said with a wink.

Mac shook his head. "Very clever."

"We best go," Joe said.

Mac followed Joe into a small market heaped with bins of brown, black, red, and white rice. They headed to the back, where a faded green curtain hung instead of a door. Joe pulled back the cloth to expose a dimly lit and musty corridor. At the end stood a stocky Chinese man with a long black queue draped over his shoulder. He guarded a carved wooden door that appeared he himself could hardly fit through.

Joe approached the man and spoke in a dialect Mac did not understand. The man shrugged his broad shoulders. Joe turned to Mac. "He knows nothing."

Mac pulled out the sealed document Shelley had given him. The man's eyes narrowed at the Nationalist's seal. He took the envelope and motioned for Mac and Joe to remain as he closed the door behind and disappeared into the next room.

Minutes later, the man returned. He signaled for

Mac to enter but stopped Joe.

Joe gave Mac an intense stare. "I no like."

"I'll be okay." He patted Joe on the shoulder.

When the door closed, someone grabbed Mac from behind. He struggled to break free but the heavy man's arm compressed his carotid artery and within seconds, he blacked out.

MAC REGAINED CONSCIOUSNESS to find himself in a chair with his shirt hanging out. He assumed his capturers had searched him. "Christ," he rubbed his neck not knowing how long he had been out. "You didn't have to knock me out."

"We needed to see if you had a weapon," said a voice from across the way.

"Try asking next time." Mac heard a growl.

The room held little light. Mac blinked numerous times then made out three silhouettes that sat behind a large table. When his eyes adjusted, he saw a man in the middle who stared at him with an ocular vacancy. The man's eyebrows curved upward like devil horns. Mac could not mistake that this was mister big himself, Du Yu-seng, a.k.a. *Big Ears Du*, leader of Shanghai's most notorious underworld organization. And seated on either side of him where two characters who looked like they could live off their body weight for a couple of weeks.

Yu-seng's voice resonated with a soft melodic tone. "You know some very influential people, Monsieur." He waved the letter in the air. "I wonder how you come to know these people."

He had forgotten to ask Shelley about the contents of the letter and wanted to kick himself for the blunder. Captive, he improvised. "I have many friends all over the world."

He saw Yu-seng nod to someone behind him. A thin man dressed in a western style black suit lumbered over to Mac and backhanded him across his cheek.

Yu-seng said, "You forget where you are. This is my house and I demand respect."

The side of his face stung and perspiration crept around his hairline. Mac scanned the room. It was windowless and the door too far for a fast getaway.

Yu-seng's eyes grew narrow and his lips pursed. "Monsieur Barnaud, what can a poor merchant, such as myself, do for you?"

Mac replied, "I need a man who can ensure safe passage for valuable shipments as they leave Shanghai's waters."

"What has that to do with me?"

"I have it on good authority that after a few

bends down the Wangpoo River, Chinese pirates board and confiscate much of the cargo. I understand you are the man to speak to about such matters."

"I might be." Yu-seng stroked his hairless chin. "What type of shipments do you refer to?"

Mac stared at Yu-seng's yellow-stained fingernails, which measured longer than seemed necessary for a man. "Opium, we're talking about large shipments of it, Monsieur."

Yu-seng examined Mac. He leaned forward and placed his elbows on the table then interlaced his thin fingers. "I think we may be able to help you," he hissed. "I've arranged a social event for business associates. There you will find someone who can assist you. I will have my associate give you directions." Yu-seng motioned to his bodyguards.

"We will meet again, Monsieur Barnaud. You have my word." A thin sinister smile formed on Yu-seng's face.

"Yeah, next time I'll be better prepared," Mac muttered.

Yu-seng's sidekicks approached Mac. They lifted him off his chair. One of the men shoved a piece of paper in Mac's jacket pocket. The other dragged him through a different door than the one he had previously entered.

A yellowish-brown haze heavy with noxious

odors of urine and feces left a bitter taste in his mouth. Lethargic Chinese as well as Europeans lay in single beds stacked four high. Some sucked on bamboo pipes like a child at a mother's breast. Others hovered over various molded glass lamps and inhaled the vaporized material. The sounds of erratic breaths echoed throughout. Death permeated the air.

Mac felt light-headed and disoriented. This was not the rice shop he and Joe had entered. A door opened letting in sunlight then one of the thugs pushed him into the street. He wiped his eyes and gagged from the tacky residue he smelled on his skin and struggled to gain his composure. He bent over, coughed out the stench from his lungs and spat a nasty wad of phlegm onto the ground, then inhaled a breath of fresh air. Before he could exhale, Mac felt the grip of someone's hand on his arm. He spun around and grabbed the man.

"Is me, Mac" Joe's face contorted. "Zowie, you look a mess."

SEVENTEEN

THE TRAIN COASTED to a stop on weed-infested track, a ways out from the North Train Station in Shanghai. Most of the station was in shambles from the 1937 bombing raids, although a few trains were still used to move to and from Nanjing.

A cold blast of wind slapped Sun across his face when he exited the train. It had been years since he had last stepped foot in this city. But today, Dai Li had ordered him to secure his opium investment and kill a man.

The buzz of street vendors, a myriad of sprint-ing rickshaw runners, and the familiar bitter taste in the air told him this was Shanghai. Except for the rumble of Japanese two-manned tanks speeding down the road, he would not have known he was in an occupied city. Sun grabbed a newspaper, folded it under his arm, and blended into the crowd.

A foul odor like that of decomposed corpses filled his nostrils when he crossed the bridge at Suzhou Creek, known to locals as *The Smelly River*. A mass of moored sampans hugged the river's edge. Along the side of their hulls bobbed rotting fish and human feces. His disgust at these Shanghailanders' disregard for hygiene made him anxious to complete his task and get out of town.

The persistent gurgle of Sun's stomach compelled him to stop beside a street vendor. He purchased a steamed bun with pungent fermented tofu, a Shanghai specialty. His first bite brought back the memory of a time during the Second Sino-Japanese War. He had worked for the Chinese Nationalists. He would sneak up on Japanese patrol soldiers and twist their necks with a deadly snap. That was before he found the pleasurable benefit of a steel knife. He enjoyed the assignment and the thrill always left him hungry for more.

The last of the day's sun was about to set when Sun arrived at the address Li had provided him. The building resided in an eclectic section of Neo-classical, Edwardian and Victorian homes known as the French Concession. The grand four-story house was set back from a stone fence. Two Bixies, lion-like mythological creatures with short wings, kept evil spirits at bay.

The skies threatened to split open as Sun walked along the circular driveway. He approached a tall red lacquered temple door where a gaunt footman dressed in traditional black tunic and pants greeted him. Inside, a triangular garden filled with trees and lush greenery filled the space. The glass ceiling gave the appearance of a conservatory. At its center was a pond with several Koi meandering among the lily pads. Sun stared mesmerized at the kaleidoscope of their white, red, orange, and black patterned scales.

The servant said, "Prosperity. Never more, never less than eight." The man pointed to the fish, "Soothsayer tell master to do."

Sun envied Yu-seng's prosperity. He followed the servant in silence down a darkened mahogany paneled hallway. Nothing hung on the walls and nothing covered a lustrous black and white tiled floor. The clackity-clack that echoed from his shoes on the tile forced him to walk on the balls of his feet to squelch the intrusive noise. He thought, it must be Yu-seng's way to detect a guest, a friend, or perhaps an intruder. He choked back his trepidation, and entered the salon.

Sun felt dwarfed by the open beamed ceiling and expansive setting. The dark red walls reminded him of dried blood. Several burnt umber leather chairs encircled a low, high-glossed onyx table. On one side of the room stood a hand-carved gilt wood screen depicting birds in flight. He turned to ask the servant a question only to find he had vanished.

Cla-clunk, cla-clunk, cla-clunk. The sound grew louder then stopped. He turned to see Du Yu-seng in the doorway. Not an exceptionally tall man, he nevertheless held an air that made one's instinct scream, DO NOT DISTURB. The most notable feature was his protruding ears. Sun diverted his eyes from them out of respect.

He shifted his weight, uneasy in Yu-seng's presence. Their last exchange had not been cordial. He had failed to kill a rival gang leader and it almost cost Yu-seng his life.

Yu-seng stepped forward and the strange sounds resumed. Sun noticed several monkey skulls that hung off the back of Yu-seng's floor length silk gown when he passed to sit down. Sun was surprised to find Yu-seng superstitious. His eyes did not waver from the skeletons until Yu-seng gestured for him to sit.

Yu-seng crossed his legs to reveal western style trousers and high quality black leather shoes. His movements were methodical as he placed his yellow stained fingers on the arms of the chair. "We have not seen you for some time, Sun."

Sun despised men that indulged in opium. "I heard about the shipload lost at sea."

Yu-seng shifted in his seat. "That was an unfortunate accident. Sometimes you get a patrol captain with high ethics who takes it under his own volition to do what he believes is right. This is war and we cannot always control these events." He cleared his throat. "Not to worry, he won't trouble us anymore."

Sun sensed Yu-seng's discomfort and realized, as Li's emissary, he was the one in control. He glared into Yu-seng's sunken bloodshot eyes. "I bring you greetings from Dai Li. He hopes business is good."

Yu-seng's thin upper lip curled. "Without this slight altercation from our island neighbors things could be better, but we manage."

"I hope for your sake you are telling the truth."

"You have my word," Yu-seng said.

Sun's eyes narrowed. "We all know about your assurances."

Yu-seng coughed into a handkerchief and wiped his nose.

Sun assumed Yu-seng required a puff of opium. "Li wants information on Japanese movements in Shanghai. He believes the enemy is building a new strategy."

"I pay our captors enough to continue operations but not enough to reveal any secrets," Yu-seng said.

"What about the Americans? Li believes they may be plotting to intrude on our trade."

Yu-seng's face looked almost the color of a corpse. "I haven't heard of anything."

"Don't you have an American on your payroll?"

Yu-seng coughed and wiped his brow. "He's a fool and knows very little."

"Have you pressed him? Sun said.

"I suppose we could . . ."

"No, let me. I know how to extract information from the unwilling."

"As you wish." Yu-seng coughed several more times. "In the meantime, someone new has joined our ranks."

"Who?"

"He's French and wants to get into the trade," Yu-seng said. "I am suspicious. I don't believe what he says. I am hosting an event tonight. Find out what you can."

Sun nodded then slid the picture Li had given him across the table. "Do you know where I can find this man?"

Yu-seng studied the picture of the occidental with light-colored hair, smiled. "It's possible he will be there tonight."

EIGHTEEN

ANYA STUFFED HER hands in her coat pockets to protect them from the cold weather. Above, leafless trees exposed empty bird nests. An overcast sky lent a gloomy backdrop. In some ways, it reminded her of a San Francisco summer day.

She passed a group of Chinese children who played a type of dice game along the sidewalk. Several of them wore padlocks attached to silver bands around their necks.

Silly superstitious parents who try to ward off evil. She sighed. To Anya the lockets had always symbolized Chinese imprisonment to their endless foreign occupation. She shrugged. *Catholics wear a St. Christopher medal for the same reason.*

In the distance, she spied a swarm of people open a path for uniformed Japanese with Arisaka rifles and bayonets. Anya stood frozen. She watched the children grab their effects and scatter. Her eyes darted around for a quick escape. She dashed down an alley and hid behind a pile of rancid garbage bins until the soldiers passed. She felt secure with the papers Shelley had given her, but the sight of their loaded rifles made her apprehensive.

The farther she traveled outside the commerce center the more desolate things looked. Entire neighborhoods had been bombed and left flattened. Piles of brick and burned out homes littered the area. She shrunk in horror at the number of beggars that swarmed the streets. Some slept, while others picked lice from their heads and skin. The pungent smell of rot drifted through the crisp winter air. *War is witness to the collapse of the human spirit.*

Anya made her way south towards the French Concession, mindful to avoid the Japanese military. She approached a familiar row of houses. Each house was two stories with several cement steps that lead up to the front door. Anya stopped across the street from Bia's last known residence. *I wonder if she still lives here.*

At the end of the block, Anya spied an elderly hunchbacked woman who wheeled a metal cart filled with packages. The woman looked familiar but a heavy coat and scarf hid much of her face.

The woman removed one of the packages and

then climbed the stairs, set the package down in front of the door then returned to gather another package. One by one, she climbed the steps and placed each package at the door. She then dragged the empty cart up the steps. The wheels hit the edge of each step until she reached the top. She returned each package to the cart then wheeled it into the house.

Anya hesitated, then ascended to the top of the stoop, inhaled, and knocked. She leaned her ear against the door. She saw a flutter from the curtain in the front window. She knocked again and heard shuffled footsteps. The door opened a crack, then further, to reveal a small craggy-faced woman dressed in black, her white hair pulled tight at the back of her head. Anya spoke in Mandarin. "Is this the home of the Chiu Family?"

The old women examined her. Anya repeated her question. "Do you have a daughter named Bia?" The woman clutched the doorframe, and her eyes welled up. Anya realized the women misinterpreted her question.

"Mamma Chiu," Anya whispered to the old woman. "It's me—Anya."

"Anya?" The woman's brow narrowed with a curious look. Her eyes opened and a smile crossed her lips. She grabbed Anya's arm and drew her inside.

"Where is Bia, Mamma Chiu?" She tried to control the excitement in her voice. "I've come a long distance to see her."

"She'll be home soon. Come, sit, have tea." The dowager hobbled in a stooped position. She had been a vibrant, talkative woman in her youth, always busy in the kitchen. Now in her late sixties to Anya she looked more like ninety. She followed her down the hallway to the kitchen.

The woman struggled to clasp the teacup with her gnarled arthritic hands. She slurped her tea and gave Anya a big smile. Anya filled her in on her life in America, up to a point. Mamma Chiu talked about her missing husband and how the family had to endure without him. Less than an hour had passed when they heard the clamor of footsteps at the front door.

Bia entered the kitchen. She wore a heavy black wrap that accented her small round ivory doll-like face. She went rigid and her skin took on an ashen color. Her black deep-set eyes darted back and forth, first to her mother then to Anya.

"Bia." Anya jumped up and moved towards her friend with open arms. She stopped when she saw Bia step back. "It's Anya. Anya Pavlovitch."

"Anya?" Bia's facial expression relaxed. "I can't believe you're back." They met in the middle of the room and embraced with a long tight hug. Anya gently stroked Bia's cheek which caused them both to tear up.

Bia removed her coat and threw it on the chair. "You may have noticed we are once again prisoners in our own city."

"Where is your papa? Your mamma kept going on about not seeing him for weeks." Anya said.

Bia lowered her voice above a whisper. "I don't want to alarm my mother. I think the Green Gang killed him for writing the truth about their activities."

Anya tried to hug Bia but she pulled away.

Bia watched her mother leave the room. "Why are you here?"

"I'm here to see you."

"No, I mean what are you doing in Shanghai?"

"I am working with a French exporter."

Bia's jaw dropped.

"A different Frenchman, that affair was over long ago," Anya said. "This is purely business. I'm assisting a French exporter who's looking to drum up some capital." She hated to lie, but she knew Bia's life could be at risk.

"Tell me about yourself. Are you married?" Anya said.

"Yes, I have a son and daughter." Bia poured herself a cup of tea.

"My mind whirls at you with kids. In some

wired way, I still see us too young to consider children." Anya laughed. Bia did not. "Where are they? I'd love to meet them."

"They're up north." She looked away. "With their father's family."

"You must miss them."

"Yes, but they are safer outside of Shanghai. The Japanese are very cruel to our young so we must do whatever is necessary to protect them."

"Yes, of course." Anya knew the torrid dislike Japanese had for any other race and that the men had no use for women, outside of their own amusement.

"What about your husband?"

"He's gone to the country on business." She walked to the other side of the room. "He has been gone longer than usual. He purchases food from country farmers to feed Shanghailanders who are unable to feed themselves or their families."

"Is your husband a communist?"

Bia shot a fierce glance at Anya. "What makes you ask that?"

"No reason, it's just that most peasants are communists or communist sympathizers and I just put it together. The communist farmers feed the starving Shanghailanders to illicit sympathy and loyalty for their cause. I recognize the tactics, it's the same ones used by Lenin."

Bia's cheeks turned rosy. "A lot has changed. We have been in a revolution for over one-hundred years, starting with the opium wars and now these recent invasions." Bia paced like an angry bee trapped and looking for a way out. "We are the rightful owners of our land. We have the inalienable right to rule our destiny and not be dictated to by any other nation."

Anya sat back in her chair.

"We've been pushed off buses by Europeans who simply wanted added room to stand, or forced to give up occupied seats." She slammed a fist into her opened hand. "We've suffered degradation and death from invaders who line their pockets from the subservient labor that they exploit. The shouts of, hey coolie, come here coolie, get this coolie, do that coolie." Bia chewed on her words. "They give us no more regard then that of an insect who crosses their path. Mao showed us that nothing in society belongs to anyone. It's the abolition of private property that will free us. You had your civil war. It's time for ours."

Anya stiffened. She remembered the strong anti-foreign movement in the late 1920s. A dangerous time when curfews where enacted. No one ventured outside the Settlement for fear of reprisals.

"You did the right thing," Bia said. "You left

China and moved to a place of your own kind," she paused. "Anya, you can't come here anymore. You put us all in danger. If we are seen together the soldiers will find a reason to take us away."

"I'm sorry I didn't mean any harm I only wanted to see an old friend. I guess I made a mistake." Ayna stepped onto the porch then turned. "Remember, I will always love you, no matter what."

Bia shut the door.

A gust of wind hit Anya straight on. She pulled her coat tight around her chest as salty tears trickled the length of her checks.

THE TRAM JOSTLED along Avenue Joffre. Red, orange, and yellow streaks painted the sky. Curfew would begin soon. She hopped off the tram and hustled down an alleyway to avoid patrols. Her heart pounded at the approach of marching men. She ducked into a sliver of a space between two buildings and inched back out of the light, and watched them pass. She trembled in the cold dark alley and wished she had left Bia's earlier.

A sudden eerie sensation consumed her. She felt a presence of another behind her. Before turned, a hand touched her shoulder. A screech burst out and she slapped her hand over her mouth.

The soldiers continued to march down the street. Their unified tread had masked her shriek. Anya looked at the dirty, ragged vagabond who held out his hand, and begged for a coin. She had nothing to give him and left him to his secret lair.

If she tried to gain entrance through the front gate, it could mean her arrest for being out after curfew. She arrived at the manhole cover only to find soldiers, who hovered around the entrance to the tunnel. She backtracked and hid in a basement stairwell. Cold and shivering, she tightened her jaw for fear someone might hear her teeth clatter. She secured her coat collar around her neck and tucked her legs close to her body to conserve heat. The smells of coal-burning furnaces and wood fireplace smoke filled the air. She longed to cuddle in front of a burning fire. She rested her head on her knees and prayed the rain would hold off. Within minutes, she had fallen asleep.

NINETEEN

CURLED UP AT the bottom of a stairwell, the rattle of a doorknob woke Anya from a fitful sleep. She jumped to her feet and adjusted her eyes to the morning sun. A brawny man opened the door. He was dressed in a sleeveless white ribbed cotton shirt splattered with bits of past meals and baggy slacks not fully buttoned. They stared at each other for a moment, then Anya dashed up the stairs. She heard the man yell after her but she refused to stop.

She arrived at the compound, presented her papers to the guard, then entered the white marble foyer. She hoped to slip into her room unnoticed but instead, she saw Mac with arms crossed, brow furrowed, and eyes blazed. She gulped. *If he were a fire-breathing dragon, I'd be reduced to ashes.*

There was a slight bruise on Mac's cheek. It looked tender. She longed to find out what happened but the fury in his eyes kept her quiet. Shelley stood next to Mac with a sheepish look on his face.

Her temples throbbed "I went to visit an old friend. What's the harm?"

"Stop." He held up one arm with his palm at her face. "I don't want to hear your excuses. I knew you'd prove yourself foolish, untrustworthy, and above all, irresponsible."

Anya dug her nails into the palms of her hands. His words cut deep. Shelley turned away and crept back to his office. She had a sudden desire to follow.

Joe entered the hall with his head in a Hardy Boys book. He looked up. Before Mac could say anything to him, Joe turned on his heels and dashed back the way he came.

Mac continued, "You're clearly not suited for this assignment. I need someone who can follow orders." He paced around with his hands on his hips. "Did you stop to think that Shelley's been sick with worry?"

"Shelley? What about you?"

"What if you had been captured? You . . ." Mac's face resembled the color of a cooked lobster.

"I . . . I . . ." She tried to explain.

"Zip it." He pinched the bridge of his nose. To Anya it seemed he wanted to squeeze her out of his thoughts. "I expect exemplary action from you. Do I make myself clear?"

She felt the burn of embarrassment and lowered her head. "Yes sir."

"Now go get cleaned up. You smell."

ANYA TUCKED HERSELF away in a small metal gray room in the basement. An undersized square wooden table and chair were all the room could hold. Overhead hung a lone bulb that flickered as though it were about to extinguish. On the desk rested a radio transmitter with telegraph key, standard issue in every American embassy.

Mac had given her a message to relay to headquarters. The scolding he gave her earlier still stung, although she remained peeved at his reaction. However, she felt it important to redeem herself.

She placed the earphones over her head and flipped the metal switch on to activate the radio then tapped out her coded message.

```
Sparrow in next.
Meeting arranged.
Information forthcoming.
```

Her other duties were to monitor Japanese movement and spot anything that might jeopardize their mission. Edmund Atwater had also given her special orders to report to him any unusual activity. She contemplated whether to contact him about Mac's meeting with the Green Gang. She recalled back when she lived in Shanghai they were ruthless gangsters who didn't play by any rules. "I'm not willing to sacrifice my life because he believes he's superman." She tapped out a message to Atwater's attention.

She rotated the large black frequency dial to listen for chatter. It took several minutes before something emerged. Dah-dit-dit-dah. She wrote down the sequence of taps. When the radio went silent, Anya removed the Wabun codebook from her satchel. A Japanese version of Morse code using dots and dashes charted in Latin letters and kana symbols. It had been the same code used to contact the Japanese Embassy in Washington on December 7.

Before she had time to complete translating the message, Atwater's reply came through:

> Don't let your prejudice blind you.
> He is a decorated naval officer.
> Rely on him with your life.

She sunk into her chair. *Everyone's against me.*

A second Japanese communication flashed.

Consumed with her thoughts, she missed the first part but jotted down the second half of the transmission. She translated the message then returned to complete the message she had been working on earlier.

```
Intern all enemy nationalists.
```

"Jesus." Her hands shook.

She had not completed relaying the message to OWI when Mac burst into the room. "Anything?"

She flung the message at him. "I think we are in serious jeopardy," she said.

"My plans had not factored in the threat of this."

"I found something else," Anya said. "I believe it's a communication from Japanese command. They are searching for a communist sympathizer they suppose is in Shanghai."

"Why?" Mac said.

"Didn't say. I wasn't able to capture the entire message. They identify him as a possible mercenary. He's using the name Sun Temujin. They're also searching for Du Yu-seng."

"Great."

"Wasn't he the man who…" She tapped her finger near her eye to indicate that she knew Yu-seng was responsible for his injury.

Mac curled his lip at her. "I'll see if Shelley can

shed some light on the gun for hire. By the way, I need you to attend a party with me this evening. I trust you can handle that?"

"I'm sure I can manage." A sudden realization crossed her mind. *I haven't anything to wear.*

TWENTY

MAC STROLLED INTO the solarium and found Shelley reading the newspaper. "With all of Miss Pavlovitch's shenanigans last night I forgot to tell you about my meeting with Du Yu-seng." Mac rubbed the side of his face, which still ached.

"I figured that things didn't go as expected from the bruise you're sport'n."

Mac smiled and fell into the wingback chair across from Shelley. "I've been invited to attend an evening affair."

"Have ya, now." Shelley peered over the top of his glasses.

"You don't seem surprised."

Shelley smiled.

"Y'all are likely to run into several British notables." Shelley folded the newspaper and sat it on his lap. "It's the only location left where dignitaries, if you can call them that, can hobnob since the Japs dismantled their beloved social clubs. It's ironic, the American social club is now the Japs Naval headquarters and the former British club is now their officers club. Isn't that a hoot?"

"Spoils of war I suppose." Mac leaned forward. "Since I have all the right papers, I think it's time my nom de plume, Rene Barnaud, gets a new address."

Shelley set his newspaper on the table. "Y'alls probably right."

"I'll need something swanky. Do you think you can get that arranged today?"

Shelley removed his spectacles and twirled them around in his fingers. "I still have a few con-nections."

"Speaking of associates . . ." Mac scanned the room. "Where's our little red-headed waif?"

Shelley held a Cheshire cat smirk. "Gone shopping I suspect."

"Was that wise? Letting her go out alone?"

"Something tells me our Miss Pavlovitch can take care of herself. Besides, I have Joe shadowing her."

"I find it difficult to believe that a skinny little boy can fend off anyone, especially soldiers."

"Joe is quite talented." Shelley strummed his fingers on the armchair. "I had him lay some things out for ya. Ya gonna need to look the part."

"How does he know my size?"

Shelley chuckled. "Joe is very good at sizing up people."

Mac shook his head. Shelley's charm made it impossible to stay mad at him for long. "Thanks. I appreciate all you're doing for us here."

"All part of the service at Shanghai Central."

Mac rose and started to leave the room then turned to Shelley. "When are you getting out of here?"

"Whadda mean?"

"How do you plan to leave Shanghai? Do you have an exit strategy?"

"I'm touched by your concern, Mac, but you needn't worry. I have many contacts to tend to my safety."

"You may need to call in favors sooner than you think."

Shelley's lips pursed. "Whadda ya saying?"

"We've received word that the Japanese plan to intern all Westerners. It might be a good idea for you to travel northwest while you still can."

"I'll be all right."

"You seem rather casual about the situation," Mac said.

"Please don't concern yourself."

"Okay," Mac said. "By the way, do you know

anyone by the name of Sun?" Mac said.

Shelley shifted in his chair. "Can't say that I do. Why?"

"We got a communication that the Japanese are in search of his whereabouts."

"It's a sure bet that if the Japs are on the hunt, they'll find him." Shelley picked up his newspaper.

Mac shrugged. "See you later."

Anya walked down Nanking Road in the heart of the International Settlement where fashionable shops once lined the street. She elbowed her way through a bedlam of crowds. Trolleys clanged, bus horns blasted, and cars honked, all vying for position through the narrow street. She noticed a few people who wore armbands with the initials "B," "A," and "N." She remembered Shelley discussing how the Japanese forced the Allied Powers, the British, Americans, and Dutch to wear armbands. "Something they learned from the Germans, no doubt. We all look alike, ya know," Shelley had commented.

She wondered about Mac's reaction to her shopping. *Would he be displeased, distressed, or simply disinterested? Pissed, I expect.*

The French were not constrained by the same rules because Vichy had given up its concessions in

China. Posing as a French expat allowed Anya more freedom to move about the city, although she was mindful of the internment message she had seen earlier regarding all Westerners. The only question that remained was when.

Familiar haunts were nowhere in sight. Many of the buildings were vacant. *Now what am I to do?* She crossed her arms at her chest. A little shop within the walled city she and her friends frequented sprang to mind. She took off again, winding along narrow side streets where laundry hung and the smell of urine permeated the air. Mindful to avoid patrols, she believed in her ability to talk her way out of a situation if stopped.

She turned the corner, caught her breath, and spotted the little dress shop five doors down. Without thought, she headed straight for the shop. Halfway down she caught sight of two soldiers wearing dull green uniforms and knee high black boots with rifles slung over their shoulders. One pulled the bill on his cloth cap up and shot her a look. They crossed the street.

She felt her pulse race. *Can't turn around. To run is out of the question. They would inevitably catch me, or worse shoot me in the back.* She decided her best bet was to continue forward.

The soldiers blocked her path and forced her to halt. Anya's heart thumped so hard she felt sure the solders could hear it. She knew it would not take much for them to drag her down an alley and violate her. One soldier removed his gun and ran the barrel across her cheek while he laughed.

"Bonjour," she quivered then gave them a polite bow and veered around them. She sensed their cold eyes on her. Pulling together bits and pieces of their conversation, she was relieved to find they were less interested in her and more concerned about finding a place to eat. She exhaled as their footsteps continued down the road.

She ducked into the dress shop and paused a moment to recover. Her mouth dropped open at the array of beautiful silk fabrics splashed across the walls. Prismatic colors of primrose pinks, mandarin oranges, jade greens, amethyst purples filled the room. There was every color imaginable with hand-woven patterns of flowers and trees and birds.

Not having time to wait for a custom fit, she tried on several ready-made dresses. Her final selection was a red silk brocade cheongsam with a bamboo and plum blossom pattern. She recalled a pair of stiletto pumps in the armoire in her room. She suspected a former resident had left them behind. *They will match perfectly with this dress.*

Package in hand, she walked out only to see a familiar face in her path. "Joe, what are you doing here?"

"Mr. Shelley ask to watch you." Joe grinned, exposing two crooked front teeth. He took the garment bag from her arms.

She felt him study her.

"Mr. Shelley tell me you live in Shanghai."

"Yes, a long time ago, but I don't like to dwell on the past." She cleared her throat. "Tell me, how did you come to work for Shelley?"

"My parents killed in '37 bombing of Chongqing. I escaped to mountains where English missionaries find me. They kind but very strict in educating us coolies." He smiled. "Not for several years did I reunite with relatives in Shanghai."

She rubbed his shoulder and thought about her parents.

"Mr. Shelley find me serving drinks at night club and tells me to come work for him. One day I save enough money to get me a swell motorcycle, like in Hardy Boys, *The Tower Treasure*."

Anya giggled. She envied his innocence.

"Why you come back?"

A smile swept away from her face. "Well . . ." Anya reflected for a moment. *It's my job . . . the war effort needed me.* She found she could not explain it even to herself. She rubbed her finger and replied, "I just missed it so." She interlinked her arm with his and they walked down the street like two girlfriends.

ANYA AND JOE returned to the embassy where she made a beeline to her room. She knew that Joe would report to Shelley about her soldier encounter and Shelley would tell Mac.

Moments later she heard Mac's raised voice reverberate from downstairs. "She did what?" echoed up the stairway. She shrugged her shoulders and continued to undress.

Mac's unmistakable footsteps caused Anya to freeze. She stood half-naked, waiting for him to burst into her room. Clomp. Clomp. Clomp—then silence. His footsteps had stopped at her door. She held her breath and stared at the doorknob. *He wouldn't dare come in.* The steps resumed down the hall then the door to his room slammed shut. She exhaled.

Why is it I stubbornly continue to go against his orders? She ran her fingers across the cheongsam dress she had laid out. *Maybe it has something to do with his need to control— everything and everybody.* "He could use a shot of vodka." She walked into the bathroom and prepared her bath.

She squeezed the sponge and let the water trickle down her back. Visions of music, gaiety, and laugher floated all-around like a dolce waltz. It had been decades since she had attended a party. Living with someone as reclusive as Paval did not allow much socializing.

She decided to pin her hair on top of her head. A pompadour hairstyle with the addition of heels would enhance her stature. The ten-inch height difference between her and Mac made her feel insignificant.

She admired her reflection in front of the full-length mirror. The close-fitting silk gown with its high neck and side-slit skirt exposed one of her legs. A pang of conceit hit her. Anya still had a beguiling figure. She twirled around the room like a small child until she got dizzy and fell on the bed. She lay there thinking about the fun she was determined to have.

A knock came at her door. "Time to go," Mac said. "I'll meet you downstairs."

Neither spoke in the cab. Anya fidgeted with her finger. Mac stared out the window.

Mac's reaction is the same as Paval when he became angry with me. She rested her head on the back of the seat and thought how similar these two men were in many ways, *perceptive and persuasive and pigheaded.* She chuckled to herself.

They weaved in and out of traffic. Large white tattered fabrics with Chinese characters painted on them were suspended from the buildings and hung over the sidewalks. The writing depicted their business from tea to brothels. Skimpily dressed girls stood near doorways. Anya felt Mac's eyes on her and wondered if he was thinking about what she had told him about her past while aboard ship.

The driver pulled over to the curb and pointed to a dimly lit alley. Anya shot Mac a look, who then turned his attention to the cabbie, who stared back at the two of them.

"I guess this is it," Mac said.

A yellow pool of light guided them down the lane. Mac scanned their surroundings then stopped when he came upon a wooden door. At its center lay the symbol of a green flag. He recalled the same logo burned onto the arm of the man who struck him. "This is the place."

"Where the hell are we?" she said.

Mac rapped twice. A peep window slid open. Beady black eyes peered out at them.

Mac held up the piece of paper that Yu-seng's men had pushed into his pocket before they dumped him onto the street.

The sounds of several locks being unhinged then the door creaked open. A small man with a ghoulish grin gestured for them to enter.

Mac moved forward while Anya remained stationary.

"Come on," Mac said.

She shook her head.

Mac took her by the arm and pulled her in. The door slammed shut. Anya jumped and grabbed

Mac's arm. "Get a hold of yourself," he whispered.

The man opened another door to reveal bright lights and the sound of music.

"I hope this place has alcohol," she said.

TWENTY-ONE

ANYA AND MAC found themselves in a small paneled room that held a freshly varnished odor. A woman stood near the cloakroom. Sounds of voices resonated from another area. Mac assisted Anya with her coat. She turned to see his intense stare at her form. A slight blush washed her cheeks and she cleared her throat.

"Don't forget to introduce me as Rene Barnaud," Mac said.

Anya rolled her eyes and grunted. "Yeah, yeah, I'm not stupid you know."

Mac took Anya by the arm and led her into the ballroom. Its immense size dwarfed the guests. The reflective sparkle from three crystal chandeliers that hung from a pseudo gilded ceiling danced off the white marble floor and mirrored walls. An eclectic group of people mingled throughout. Several

Europeans huddled together on one side of the room. Opposite them sat Chinese men dressed in traditional tunics and pants playing mahjongg. Anya spotted several Chinese men wearing western attire with garish dressed women clinging to their arms. She assumed they were gangsters and their molls. Meanwhile, frustrated musicians played against a backdrop of loud voices.

"Let's dance," Mac said. Before Anya could respond, he had taken her in his arms. "I want to listen in on some conversations." He held her so tight she had trouble breathing. *Guess he's still upset with me.* She squirmed and he relaxed his grip.

"Where did you learn to dance? Back on the farm?"

"My older sister liked to dance to country music on the radio when I was a kid."

Anya smiled at the image of him and his sister.

They slowly spun about the dance floor while the band played a rendition of Hoagy Carmichael's "Stardust." Mac relaxed his grip on her. The gentle warmth of his hand felt pleasurable against her back. An image of Paval flashed before her. She suffered a twinge of disloyalty to his memory and stiffened.

They glided past a couple. The Chinese woman spoke about a possible movie role. Another couple conversed in Russian. Unable to understand, Mac asked Anya for assistance. She chuckled then exhaled. "He's trying to get the woman to go to bed with him."

She thought she saw a streak of color across his cheeks, yet his eyes seemed distracted by something.

From behind her, a baritone voice said, "Anya, *ma amour*,"

Mac released her and Anya spun around. It took her a moment to recognize the person. She felt a sting in her heart as though someone gripped it and her knees almost gave way.

"Guy Gilot." It had been more than twelve years since they were last together. "I can't believe my . . ." She lost her voice.

Guy was tall with sandy-blond hair mingled with traces of gray. He had an athletic build that men envied and women lusted. He kissed her lightly on both cheeks and drew her away from Mac and spun her around. *"Ma chérie*, you look marvelous. But then you never fail to please a man's eye."

Anya saw Mac's jaw clench.

"You're too kind," she said. "Let me introduce you to Maaa . . . Monsieur Rene Barnaud."

"Enchanté de faire votre connaissance, *Monsieur."* Guy greeted Mac, though his eyes never left Anya.

"Merci, Monsieur. Le plaisir, c'est à moi . . ." Mac's voice trailed off as Guy ushered Anya away. He stood dumbfounded that she had left without a word, but not surprised. "I'm taller," he said.

Mac kept a watchful eye on them. He was still irritated from the earlier episode with the Japanese soldiers. He gritted his teeth. *What the hell else can interfere with this mission?*

He sauntered over and joined the Europeans in conversation. They were a mix of British, French, and Dutch businessmen who all had an affiliation with the underworld. Mac inquired about Du Yu-seng.

"Oh—he never attends his own parties," piped up a stocky Englishman. "These are the perks he offers to his best clients." The man winked.

"Yu-seng's most likely gambling at the mahjongg tables at a private residence," someone interjected. "His addictions are multifaceted." They all laughed.

"Mr. Barnaud, what is your business here in Shanghai?"

"Shipping," Mac replied.

The group of men sneered at one another. One man slapped Mac on the shoulder and cackled, "Good luck my boy." Another said, "You'll need it."

He wondered whether to warn them about the

possible mass internment, but if he did he would expose his cover. Instead, he focused his attention on Anya and Guy who headed towards the bar. He worried that her drinking might affect not only her judgment but loosen her tongue.

Before he could reach them, an ugly little fellow with a visible scar across his hairline stood in Mac's path. He wore a tight fitting double-breasted suit with wide lapels and a patterned necktie.

"Monsieur Barnaud?" he said.

"*Oui.*" Mac noted a ring that glistened while the man twirled his cane.

"Let me present myself. I am Sun Temujin." Sun gave a slight bow then leered at a woman with a low cut gown who passed.

Mac remained calm but his mind raced to remember why the name rang familiar. It was the name from the message Anya had intercepted. However, this person did not resemble other Chinese. This fellow had thick coarse black hair that stuck out in several directions and black eyes that resembled gashes.

"Mr. Yu-seng insisted that we get together to discuss some business." Sun fondled his cane.

"I don't like to mix business with pleasure," Mac said.

"Yes, you are correct—not the right place to speak of such—a sensitive matter," Sun hissed.

"Let's say tomorrow 10:00 a.m. at the Cathay Hotel," Mac said.

"Good—till tomorrow then."

Sun walked out the door twirling his cane.

ANYA AND GUY stood near the bar amongst the other guests who waited for their drinks. The bartender created old-fashioneds, manhattans, and martinis like a circus juggler. Behind the bar hung an elaborate woodcarving of a coiled snake with half its body erect and a sharp-toothed rat poised to strike each other. A crescendo of voices made it difficult to carry on a conversation.

"I've missed you," Guy said.

"What?" Anya held one hand to her ear with a coy smile.

"I said, would you like a drink?"

"Will you be there in the morning?" They both laughed. Years prior, he had taken her to a high-end restaurant where they had shared a bottle of champagne. The next day he left Shanghai and she never saw him again.

"White lighting is it?" Guy winked then turned to the barkeep and ordered two shots of vodka.

She downed the vodka and asked the bartender for a second.

"Feeling feisty tonight are we?" he said.

"Wicked day— just need a little something."

Guy took her by the hand and escorted her out of the ballroom. She noticed Mac across the way speaking to someone whose back was to her.

"Where are we going?" she said.

"Somewhere secluded." He moved his eyebrows up and down.

They entered a small soft-lit library where every bit of wall space held a book. The warmth from burning logs lent a romantic ambiance to the room. The noise level had tempered to a low buzz.

"This should do," he said.

They sat down on the chesterfield positioned in front of the fire. "Why did you ever leave me?" he said.

Resting her head on the back of the couch, she stared into the blaze. "If I recall correctly, you left me." She turned and caught his inviting gaze. Those warm brown eyes that always lay half-open imparting a sultry, sensual, sexy appearance. He leaned in but she spun away.

"When your government calls you in to help Chiang Kai-shek assimilate western culture you can't simply refuse," he said.

Anya crinkled her nose at him.

"Who's the spook?" Guy said.

"You mean Bernaud?" She smiled. "He's a French importer."

"If he's a Frenchman, I'm a Limey."

"Do I hear jealousy?"

A familiar Gershwin tune drifted into the room. Her mind slipped back to a time when she was having tea with friends. Guy had entered the restaurant and everyone's head turned. He was tall and dapper with a trace of gray around his temples. He invited her to dinner with an assuredness she had never encountered before. That night, she told him the truth regarding her lifestyle but he seemed dismissive. Others had not been so generous. One escort sent her to the hospital with a broken collarbone and serious bruises. They lived together for several months but she never returned the same intense affection he held towards her. She wondered if he still retained those same feelings.

She twisted her finger without thought.

"I see you haven't lost your twitch." His eyes pointed to her finger. "Why don't you put a ring on that finger?" he said.

"There is only one ring that fits this finger."

"Do you think you'll ever find it?"

"It's my earnest hope." She sighed.

He pulled her towards him and she released all her tension and nestled against his brawny body. She felt safe and glad to have him back in her life. She knew he was someone she could rely on if things got nasty.

A cold draft wafted across the side of her face, and she heard somebody clear their throat. Anya turned to see Mac standing in the doorway. His brow formed a familiar V indicating his continual displeasure with her.

Guy whispered in her ear. "Tomorrow. Shanghai Tea House. Two o'clock. Don't be late." She kissed him on both cheeks then left with Mac.

Mac fidgeted with his gloves as they waited outside for a cab. Anya thought about how little Guy's physical appearance had changed. *He is as handsome as ever.* She started to hum.

"Exactly who is Guy Gilot?" Mac said. "One of your . . ." He stopped himself.

Anya pulled her collar up. "I knew him a long time ago. We were—friends." She grinned inwardly.

"What does he do?"

"Do? Well, he's sort of a French version of you."

"What the hell is that suppose to mean," he said.

"He knows lot of secrets." Mac turned to meet her glare. "For example he knows you're not who you say you are." He shifted his weight back and forth. "Don't worry, he's not going to tell anyone. He's one of the good guys."

"Oh yeah. I could tell from the Good Guy tattoo on his forehead. What . . ." He stopped speaking when the taxi arrived.

He directed the cabbie to take them to the Cathay Hotel. Anya knew enough not to say anything that the driver might overhear. She looked at Mac who refused to turn her way. She wondered why a hotel and not to the consulate. Mac's crossed arms meant she was in for another lecture.

They rode in silence. She stared out the window as they passed by a wooden hexagon Confucian temple with an intricate roofline. Each corner of its pagoda shape curved upward, exposing its underbelly, reminiscent of a graceful bird. She thought how wonderful it would be to fly away from Mac.

At the hotel, they walked toward the registration desk. Mac said, "You're going to have to stay here tonight. I can't afford to have anyone follow us to the embassy now that I have made contact."

Anya nodded. She noticed his fisted hands.

They were silent in the elevator. The bellman whistled a simple tune. Anya thought it was his way of cutting the obvious tension. She felt her throat tighten as though Mac had hold of it.

Mac tipped the bellman and closed the suite door. He made his way towards Anya and grabbed her arm then threw her onto the bed. She landed so hard she believed her dress had split.

"Damn it. If you've ripped my . . ."

"You have reunited with a woman from your past and now this man. Who else can we expect? You can't trust anyone, especially the French. Vichy is in league with the devil."

"He's not the enemy," she said. The vein in Mac's neck bulged out so far it looked like it would burst. *I know he's killed a woman. I wonder if she made him mad.*

He paced around then yelled, "What did you tell Guy about me?"

"I didn't say anything to him." She shook from fear but mostly out of anger.

"Then how does he know I'm not legit?"

She tried to stand up but he pushed her down. "I don't know." she screamed. "Maybe your terrible French accent convinced him."

"Why is every conversation between us a competition that you must win?" he said.

"Okay then you're right, right, right, right, right." She stuck her bottom lip out.

"It's not about winning, it's about surviving. What were you thinking going off on your own today?" he paused. "You're, you're like the eye of a typhoon and anyone who gets near you is caught up in your spiral."

He paced again. "You put me in danger. You put Shelley in danger. You put yourself in danger. If we fail because of your inability to follow the simplest of orders it will be on your head."

"You forget that I know my way round this town and I am accustomed to dealing with dangerous situations." She twisted her finger at the lie. "Guy won't betray me."

Mac threw his hands up in the air. "How do you know?"

"We have a bond, the kind that lasts a lifetime."

"Don't be naïve. People change over time."

"Not Guy."

"What makes you so sure?"

"Because—he's in love with me." She pulled herself off the bed and marched into the bathroom to check her dress.

TWENTY-TWO

M AC THOUGHT OF ways to hogtie Anya and ship her back home as he adjusted his charcoal gray worsted wool jacket. Her disappearance earlier that morning had him exhausted.

There was a hard rap at the door. He had not expected his visitor early. *Punctual bastard.* He adjusted his silk tie in the mirror and took a deep breath before opening the door.

"Bonjour, Monsieur Sun." Mac motioned him into the room. Sun wore a blue double-breasted suit with wide stripes and a flamboyant multi-colored ascot. Sunlight pierced through the blinds and reflected off a pink jade tiepin. Mac snickered under his breath at the garish attire. "Have a seat. Would you like coffee or tea?"

"No thank you." Sun sat in a ladder-back chair

and twirled his elaborate silver-capped cane. "Yu-seng tells me you need protection for your shipments."

"That's what I like," Mac said with a one-sided grin. "A man who gets right down to business." He poured himself a cup of coffee, careful to keep one eye on Sun. Mac sat in the chair across from him. "What assurances can you give me I'll receive my goods intact?"

Sun cleared his throat. "We can only guarantee the safety of your cargo on the Huangpu River." Sun's eyes narrowed. "Once your shipment reaches the Yangtze River Delta our influence ends."

Mac took a sip of his drink and studied his opponent, who appeared relaxed, almost smug. Sun twisted an opulent ring on his finger. Mac remembered the ring from last night and thought it looked too delicate for a man's hand but somehow it fit this man's persona. "Your influence ends? What does that mean?"

"From Shanghai to the delta is under Yu-seng's control. However, from the delta to the sea is under another's."

Mac placed his cup on the table. "Then it's imperative I meet the person who controls those waters. If I am going to pay top yuan, I want total protection."

Sun's face flashed red. He slammed the metal

butt of his cane on the floor. "No one commands an audience with Dai . . ." He caught himself and sat back in his seat.

Mac suppressed a smile. He knew Sun referred to Dai Li, the head of secret police for Chiang Kai-shek. He had made this trip to Shanghai for one reason. His orders were specific—kill Dai Li.

"I believe Li will want to meet with me." Mac crossed his legs and rested his arms on the chair arms.

Sun settled back in his seat with a smirk on his face. "What makes you so certain?"

"We're talking about a lot of money. Money that will preserve Li's power." Mac rose slowly, walked over, and opened the door. "Until I can speak to Li, we have nothing further to discuss."

Sun stood and tightened his grip on his cane. Mac was prepared to take him on if necessary. Sun lowered his cane as he neared the door.

Sun's jaw clenched and he ground his teeth. "I'll get back to you."

"Tomorrow. No later." Mac shut the door, relaxed his shoulders, and heaved a sigh of relief. He picked up his cup. The liquid sloshed from a slight tremble in his hand. He downed the lukewarm java.

His thoughts returned to Anya. *I wonder where that prickly pear has gone off to.*

TWENTY-THREE

MAC HAD FORBIDDEN Anya from further contact with Shelley and the embassy, but she felt compelled to return, if only to retrieve the codebook. This was something Mac either forgot or did not place importance on. Her mind weighed heavily on concerns regarding Mac's involvement with local gangsters. Even though the message from Edmund Atwater told her to trust Mac's judgment, she could not dismiss her uncertainty. She decided to ask for Guy's help.

Anya heard Shelley in conversation as she walked down the hall of the consulate. "Ya, I have it right here. Don't worry, I have everything under control." He placed the receiver in its cradle when she entered the office.

"Anya," he said as he slid a piece of paper in his top desk drawer. "I'm surprised to see y'all here. I assumed you and Mac wouldn't be back again."

"I wanted to pick up some of my things."

"I sent everything over," he said.

"Um, I'm missing an item."

"Can I help?"

"No, no. I'll only be a moment."

"Well, I am glad y'alls here. Mac seemed concerned about my plans. I wanted to let him know that Joe and I are leaving for Yan'an. It's . . ."

"I know where Yan'an is—it's up north." She frowned. "Aren't Mao Zedong and his communist troops up there?"

He shifted in his chair. "We'll be safer with them than anyone else during these turbulent times." He shuffled papers on the desk. "It's best if ya don't return here again. I'm not positive but I believe someone is watching the place."

Anya nodded. "When do you plan to leave?"

"Soon."

"Is everything all right?"

"Hunky-dory."

She left and climbed the stairs to her room. Waves of sadness swept over her at the thought of never seeing Shelley again. In the short time they had known each other, she had come to enjoy his charismatic and warm qualities. She would miss him.

Anya shoved her hand under the mattress and

removed the hidden book. She placed it in the bathtub and struck a wooden match. The flammable material of the codebook ignited and turned into a mound of ash in seconds. She turned on the faucet and washed the evidence down the drain. *Bad days are ahead I can feel it.* She bit her bottom lip and rubbed her finger. *Hold it together girl. Don't let fear consume you.*

On her way out, Anya passed by Shelley's office. She noticed his hands cupped over his face. "What's the matter?"

He raised his head. "I just had a phone call. The editor of the Chinese Press died from his wounds. The Japs must have done a real number on him."

"You said the Chinese Press. Who?"

"Xing Chiu."

She gasped with a whisper. "Bia's papa"

"Did y'all know him?"

"No, it's just such awful news." She lied. "Good fortune to you and Joe."

She bolted out the front door. A few yards away Joe was leaning against a tree. He raised his hand as if to wave then put it down. She wanted to say goodbye but was already inexcusably late.

THE MAITRE D' ESCORTED Anya through a tranquil garden. The air held a fresh floral scent after the recent rain. The spatter of water came from a small waterfall where a statue of a white Buddha sat to one side. They crossed a bamboo footbridge to a private pavilion. The modest room held a single table and four chairs. The windows held no glass; instead of a solid door there hung a red drape.

Guy rose from his seat when Anya entered. She admired Guy's impeccable appearance from his coifed blond hair down to his polished black shoes. A warm flutter tickled her stomach. His face radiated a sensual glow that she remembered from times past.

"Sorry, I'm late. Have you been here long?" she said.

He kissed her on both cheeks, then one more time and pulled a chair out for her. "Not long," he replied.

"That must be one proficient chef." She looked at the table laden with various dim sum plates and a pot of hot tea.

He smiled and sat beside her rather than across from her. "I've made arrangements so we won't be disturbed."

Anya popped a small dumpling into her mouth. "Sorry, but I am so hungry." She covered her mouth with her hand. "You said you had something for me."

"Daylight does you justice, my dear," he said.

She sensed heat rise in her cheeks.

"You're even prettier when you smile. Have some tea." He filled her cup then his own. "You're not here by accident."

"I know, it's kismet." She leaned in and a wisp of hair fell across her forehead.

He brushed it to the side "Not exactly, you were sent to me."

"You mean the angels led me to you."

"No, Edmund Atwater."

"What are you saying?"

"Atwater couldn't possibly come himself."

She shook her head, "No, wait. I am here to assist . . ." She caught herself.

Guy drew a broad smile. "I don't know what that French imposter is doing here but you were sent here to meet me."

Anya sucked in a breath of air. "What are you saying? Mr. Atwater tricked me into coming here?"

"Let's say persuaded you."

"What?" Her lips puckered. *I am disgusted with men lying to me. I just can't trust any of them.*

She fell against the back of her chair and twisted her finger to calm herself. Atwater did leave the decision to her, she thought. Although that was arguable. Since her arrival, she felt more in control, more confident, less of a pushover.

"Why me?"

"You were the best possible link. We knew each other and it seemed less suspicious from prying eyes to reunite with someone from my past."

Her jaw dropped. "You're G^2." She remembered handing Atwater the decoded message only a week ago.

Guy smiled and nodded.

"But the message said your life was in danger."

"My life is always in danger." He kissed the inside of her hand.

A tingle traveled the length of her body. "How, do you know Atwater? How did you know I would come?" She tried to slow her delivery. "How does any of this make sense?"

"Atwater and I became friends several years ago while in Jakarta. He's one of the few people that I trust with my life. I can't trust the Vichy government here, so I contacted him."

"I just can't get over you and Atwater." Anya failed to notice Guy remove something from his pocket.

"I have something for you." He swung the object in front of her face.

Her eyes focused on an inlaid gold locket. "What is it?"

"Something very special." He fastened the chain around her neck.

"Expensive by the look of it." She ran her

fingers over the raised surface, her face twisted. "A snake's head?"

"It's a Pit Snake," he said. "They are extremely venomous and known for their cunning ambush behavior. It's not the piece that is priceless, but what it holds. It's information on Chiang Kai-shek's recent ties with Japan. You must guard this with your life. Give it to Edmund Atwater upon your return to America."

She continued to admire the locket.

"Anya." His tone bellowed like a military order.

"Yes. Yes." She sat at attention.

"Tell no one, understand?"

"Yes, I heard you. Since we're being serious, I need a favor." Anya took a deep breath. "This morning Mac, that's his real name . . ."

"I would have guessed Biff or Bucko," Guy said.

"Anyway," she said, "He confessed to me that he was meeting someone named Sun Tem . . ."

"Sun Temujin?"

"Have you heard of him?"

"He is treacherous and well known in certain circles as a mercenary, but no one will admit to hiring him. Rumor has it he was in Russia working with the Red Army, possibly Lenin himself. He disappeared after Lenin's death and resurfaced in Nanking when Chiang took over. I am not sure whom he works for now. But it doesn't bode well for Mac's survival if he's linked with Sun."

She wiped the crumbs from the corner of her mouth with her napkin and returned it to her lap. "Mac's already met with Du Yu-seng and now Sun. I fear he may be in over his head." She sighed. "Behind enemy lines in Europe is one thing, but this is Shanghai."

"Yeah, this place is a Mecca for espionage." Guy nodded. "Sun has no known affiliations. He could be working for the Communists, or the Nationalists, or both."

A cold chill crawled up her neck. "That's why I need your help."

"I don't see how I can be of assistance."

"Can't you follow Mac and watch his back?"

"Why should I risk my neck for him?"

"For me, do it for me. I was a real mess when I left Shanghai. America took me in when I had nothing. The success of this mission is my chance to repay the debt and honor my father's memory."

Guy rested his hand on Anya's arm. "Are you in love with this chap?"

Anya sat upright. "With Mac?" She rolled her eyes. "God—no."

"For you then, I'll do it for you." His voice trailed off and he leaned close to her face.

Anya heard a faint whizz, like a swarm of locust

in the distance, then a thud. They both turned around. Imbedded in the back of Guy's chair hung a large knife. Guy yelled at Anya to get under the table then he ran out.

She scrambled under the table and wrapped her hands around one of its legs.

Moments later Guy returned. "I didn't see anyone but we need to go."

Anya still crouched under the table. "Was that meant for you or me?" Her lower lip quivered.

"Not sure," he said.

Her body trembled as Guy helped her up. He cradled her in his arms and whispered in her ear. "I'll take you somewhere safe."

NEITHER OF THEM took notice of the flash of light or the rain that beat against the window like rhythmic drums. Anya stood near the fireplace. She twisted her finger and watched small flames dance around the log. Guy removed a seventy-eight record from its jacket and placed it on the RCA turntable. A melodious French cabaret song resonated throughout the apartment.

He poured two drinks and handed one to Anya. "*Longue durée de vie*."

"*Dasvidania*," she replied.

They clinked their glasses. She downed the

vodka. He matched her movement, followed by a coughed, "Should we smash the glasses in the fireplace?" he said.

She smiled and faced the flame.

Guy stood behind her, placed his hands on her shoulders, and then walked his fingers down her arms. His fingertips felt like little sparks of electricity on her skin.

He whispered in her ear, "Everything will be fine. Don't worry Love."

She turned to face him and saw a fierce hunger in his eyes. She nestled her cheek against his collarbone and smelled the aroma of sandalwood and jasmine. A bittersweet taste hung on her lips when she kissed his neck. She surrendered into his safe and familiar arms.

"I never stopped thinking about you," he whispered. He pulled her chin up to meet his lips. Her body quivered and wilted all at the same time. He wrapped his arms around her waist and drew her in tight. His tongue penetrated deep into her mouth and she released a soft moan. She drew back and clawed his shirt open to touch his skin.

Guy found the tear in her dress from the other night and tugged on it. She tilted her head to look up at him and felt her eyes glaze. He unhinged his jaw like a python and devoured her mouth. Sliding his hand in the slit of the dress, he ripped it further.

His hand traveled to her bare derriere. He grabbed a handful of flesh and squeezed hard. Anya let out a yelp and dug her nails into his back.

She broke their embrace, unbuckled his belt, pulled it though each loop, and then massaged his erection. He tore the dress off her body. She stood nude, in a pair of black stilettos. He kissed one milk-pale breast then the other, sliding his tongue over her pink nipples until they hardened. His hand glided down the curve of her hip then between her legs. A coo bubbled up to her lips.

He held a fervent kiss on her lips, picked her up with one swoop then carried her into the bedroom.

TWENTY-FOUR

ANYA HEARD GARBLED voices as she approached Mac's hotel suite. She wondered if Sun was in the room. Her fingers poised on the doorknob, she flashed on what Guy told her about him—Sun is despicable and not to be trusted. She hesitated for several seconds then went in. She stopped short at the sight of Mac and Joe sitting and drinking coffee like two old friends.

"Nice of you to join us this afternoon," Mac said. "Where have you been for the last twenty-four hours?"

Anya avoided looking in Mac's direction, but sensed his wicked stare on her. She sauntered over to the other side of the room and flopped down in the chair next to Joe.

She watched Joe's eyes trail down to her

neckline. "That's sure a swell piece of jewelry," he said.

"Thank you," she said.

"A snake, how befitting," Mac said.

She fondled the locket and ignored Mac's remark. "I thought you and Shelley were leaving for Yan'an?"

Joe's eyes darted to Mac.

"Shelley is dead," Mac said. "No doubt, murdered."

"Jesus." Anya sat upright. It had only been hours ago when she had last seen his cherub face. She gave Joe a sympathetic look and patted his hand. "I'm so sorry, Joe."

Joe pulled away and shifted in his chair. She felt slighted but let it pass.

"How?" she said.

"Joe found him slumped over his desk this morning."

Anya picked up a half-filled glass and took a sip then choked, "What is this?"

"Last night's bourbon," Mac said.

"I need vodka."

"Try the bar," Mac pointed.

Anya poured a good amount of vodka in a glass and knocked it back in one gulp. "Why would anyone want to kill Shelley?" She directed her question to Joe who shifted his eyes away from her.

"I can think of a hundred reasons, and each one includes you," Mac said.

"Me?"

"Your insolence is beyond redemption. I told you not to return to the embassy. You simply can't be trusted. I'm sure someone followed you there."

"No one followed me."

"How can you be sure?"

Anya tightened her hand into a fist and walked across the room to where Mac sat. She was close enough to smell his rancid coffee breath. She shouted. "You blame me for Shelley's death?" Her face flushed from the alcohol. "While you've been exposing yourself to every gangster in Shanghai, I've been trying to improve our chances of getting out of here alive."

"With whom—the Frenchman?" Mac snapped.

Anya whacked Mac across his cheek with a force that made his head jerk back. He jumped out of his seat. A red outline of her fingers remained on his face.

Both toe to toe, her chin turned up to meet his eyes. She could see his nostrils flair. "No matter how clever you think you are, don't think for a moment you can pull this off alone."

Before he could refute her, there was a knock at the door. "Both of you get in the bedroom and keep quiet," Mac said.

Anya waggled her finger at Mac. "If that's Sun, you'd better be careful."

He waved her into the other room without responding. "Who is it?" Mac said.

"I have a message for Monsieur."

Anya closed the bedroom door. "Joe." She placed her palm on his shoulder. He moved, which caused her hand to fall away.

"I can't tell you how sorry I am. Shelley always treated me with respect and kindness." She tried to coax him to look at her but he turned away and hung his head. "I would never do anything to jeopardize either of your lives. I'm sure I wasn't followed."

In a low voice he said, "It's not your fault."

She bit her bottom lip. *Why won't he look at me?*

"You can come out now," Mac yelled.

Anya watched Mac shuffle around the room. He wrung his hands and cleared his throat like a nervous schoolboy.

"I appreciate all that you have done, Miss Pavlovitch. I know there are things I couldn't have done without your assistance but it's time to go our separate ways. I feel I need to complete this mission alone."

"Really." She placed her hands on her hips. "And just what to do you expect me to do?"

"We've been talking," he pointed to Joe. "We

think it best if you left Shanghai."

She frowned and tried to speak, but Mac intervened.

"It would be safer for you to accompany Joe up north. There you can hook up with the local government and arrange passage back to the States."

Anya remembered what Guy said—your objective is to insure safe delivery of this vital information. She relaxed and swallowed her anger. Sudden remorse swept through her for the slap that still lay red on Mac's cheek.

She spotted a slip of paper on the table that had not been there before. She squeezed the snakehead and acquiesced, "I agree."

Mac's mouth fell open.

TWENTY-FIVE

A LIGHT MIST swept across Anya's face as she followed several steps behind Joe. She unfolded the paper that she had palmed off the table in Mac's suite. It read:

> *The party you wish to meet will be at*
> *North Railway Station tomorrow,*
> *11:00 p.m.*

She stopped and reread the message.

Joe turned around and said, "Come Miss Anya, no dillydally. Uncle's shop just ahead. There we find you safe passage up north."

Anya frowned. "Joe, when you say up north, do you mean the communists?"

Joe stammered, "Ah, yeah."

I'd rather take my chances in Shanghai than trust communists.

Joe took Anya to a backroom of the teahouse.

"I be back," Joe said with a bow. "I go find Uncle."

Scattered on a long, worm-holed table rested a mosaic of stacked herbs used to blend various teas. She lingered over a heap and drew in the fragrance. The dried fibers that smelled like dead grass filled her nose and made her wheeze, then cough. She stepped back, sneezed several times into her sleeve and massaged her nose.

She thought about sneaking out when she heard voices. She placed her ear against the closed door. They were speaking a Chinese dialect she understood. "What am I suppose to do with her?" a man's voice grumbled.

"Some people are coming to take her." Joe's voice sounded several octaves higher than normal. "You know what to do Uncle. We have no choice. They already killed Mr. Shelley, you're next."

I've got to get the hell out of here. She exhaled slowly to calm her racing heart. *This couldn't have been Mac's plan.*

She heard footsteps walk away and assumed Joe left. She started for the doorknob then noticed it turn. She stepped back. An old man shuffled into the room. He seemed close to her height, albeit bent over. She moved one foot forward, poised to attack. The uncle recoiled. A burly younger man appeared in the doorway. He stepped towards her with his arms extended like the monster in

Frankenstein. She pulled herself back.

"You need to come with us," the uncle said.

"I need to go to the bathroom," she blurted out.

He nodded to the younger man.

The bathroom had a small open window shy of arms reach. She jumped. Her fingertips brushed the windowsill. A commotion stirred outside the door. "Just a minute," she called out.

She crouched before she jumped again. Her fingers grabbed the windowsill but her hands were too wet from sweat to secure a grip.

She wiped her palms on her trouser legs and tried again. This time she secured a tight grip and hoisted herself up. Placing one elbow then the other, she struggled to pull herself through the opening. Her upper body hung out the window. She stopped to catch her breath. Two stories down was a large trash bin.

The doorknob rattled. She plunged face first onto a large pile of garbage. A nasty bitter pungent stench filled her nostrils and she gagged. She felt around her neck. The necklace was gone. *It must have caught on the sill and popped off.* She fell to her knees desperate to find it.

From above, Anya heard someone shout, "She's outside in the trash."

Black snake eyes peered down at her. Bits and

pieces of litter flew in the air as her frantic search continued. "God, please help me." Something pinched her left breast. She fished her hand down her blouse, pulled out the locket, and kissed it. "Thank you."

The old man's sidekick rounded the corner. She slid down the pile of trash. She could almost feel his breath on her as she ran down the alley. When she reached the street, Anya jumped in front of a bus that almost clipped her heels. She bent over, hands on her knees, mouth agape and sucked in oxygen. The smell of burnt rubber filled the air.

The maneuver had placed distance between her and the hunter, allowing her time to think. The clang of a streetcar grabbed her attention and she leapt onboard. Panting, crouched in her seat, the trolley pulled away. She watched her pursuer dart about in search of her.

TWENTY-SIX

T HE TELEPHONE IN Mac's suite rang. He had
not expected a phone call. *It's probably Joe about
Anya refusing to leave.* He smiled. *Perhaps she drowned in
the river or got squashed by a rickshaw.* The phone
continued to sing out.

He stretched his arm for the receiver.

"Mac, it's Joe."

He ground his teeth. "Did Anya get off all
right?"

"Ah, yeah. She good. Uncle take her up north
like you say."

He sighed in relief. "Why didn't you go?"

"You meet me in fifteen at tea shop?"

"What about?"

"Can't say over phone."

"Okay, but make it twenty." He went into the
bathroom and splashed cold water on his face. He

rubbed his stubble and debated whether to shave. He thought better of it and rushed to put on his jacket and hat then raced to catch the elevator.

AFTER SEVERAL BLOCKS, Mac heard the even footsteps from behind. He stopped in front of a shop window. Out of the corner of his eye, he spotted Guy pretending to read a newspaper. He remembered seeing a man reading in the hotel lobby. But the paper covered his face. "That bitch."

Mac tried to pick up his pace but the crowd rendered him almost immobile. He made a quick dash into a barbershop. He passed a man sitting on a stool getting his head shaved, another man sat waiting. The barber held his blade at Mac and screamed something in Chinese. Mac ran to the back, where he found an exit to the alley.

Mac heard the barber scream again before the back door slammed shut. He ran down the alley then took a hard right. Mac's speed caused his hat to fall off his head. Not having the time to retrieve it with Guy moments behind, he ducked into a clothing store. Hidden behind a rack of western style trousers, Mac pushed apart the clothes just enough to see Guy pick up his fallen hat. Guy focused on the shop. Mac saw Guy's burning eyes scan the area. He waited, ready to attack if Guy ventured in. Guy took a step into the shop then hesitated, tossed the hat and sped down the street. Confident he had eluded Guy, Mac rushed down the other way.

Mac had not gone more than a half a block when a large overweight man with thick black hair and sliver thin lips grabbed him by the arm. Mac punched the man in the stomach. The man barely blinked. Mac went to hit him again but the man caught his fist and twisted Mac around then shoved him in the back of a black sedan

Mac found himself sandwiched between Yu-seng and the large thug.

"We meet again," Yu-seng hissed. With a slow wave, he motioned for the driver to go. "I understand you're unhappy with our arrangements."

"I wouldn't say unhappy. I just don't believe you can give me everything I need. My concerns are for my cargo in open waters, which I've been told is out of your control," Mac said.

"So much water. So little protection. What to do?"

"I've been informed that there is someone whose influences extend beyond yours," Mac said.

"You refer to the great Dai Li." Yu-seng ran his fingers down the crease of his pant leg. "Would you like to meet him? Of course, you would." Yu-seng sneered. "Why?"

A surge of adrenaline kicked in. Mac sized up his options but there was no room to maneuver, let alone make a quick exit. "I believe Li is the link I need to secure my cargo's safe passage."

"I don't think you care about any cargo. What do you think, Yoyo?" Yu-seng leaned forward to look at the thug. "Does our friend here seem concerned about opium?"

Yoyo laughed, exposing several missing teeth and breath that made Mac's eyes water.

"I think you want very much to meet Li. Why?" Yu-seng tapped his bony fingers on Mac's leg. "I'm curious."

Mac tried to swallow but he had no spit. "As I said . . ."

Yu-seng continued. "I believe you're in Shanghai for reasons altogether more sinister. Murder perhaps?"

Mac did not see the wooden dowel that Yoyo pulled out from his inside coat pocket. The impact of the rod hit him in the stomach. He felt it all the way to his backbone. He doubled and let out a guttural groan. He gasped for air. Then he felt a crushing blow to his skull. Before he lost consciousness, he whispered, "Damn . . . Joe."

TWENTY-SEVEN

ANYA SNUCK AROUND to the back of Bia's house. She climbed two steps and knocked on the door. Footsteps approached then the door opened. Anya was surprised to see a tall Chinese man dressed in a tan cotton shirt and pants.

"Is Bia at home?" Her voice quivered through the screen door.

He said nothing and turned around leaving the door open.

Bia scowled from the other side of the mesh. She wore similar styled clothing as the man. Anya thought it must represent some type of uniform.

"I told you never to come here," Bia said.

"I have something important to tell you."

"There is nothing you have to say that interests me."

"It's about your baba. Please let me come in."

Bia shot a look at the man next to her. He nodded and walked away. She waved Anya inside.

"The gentlemen, is he your husband?" Anya said.

"What do you have to say?" Bia said.

Anya did not wait for an invitation and sat at the kitchen table. She felt her stomach knot up when she relayed what Shelley had informed her about Mr. Chiu and his blackened feet. "It appears your papa died from his wounds received at the hands of the Japanese."

The stiffness in Bia's body gave way and she collapsed into the chair next to Anya. Her face fell into her cupped hands and she sobbed. Anya rubbed Bia's shoulder.

"I am sorry to bring you such disheartening news but I knew you'd want to know," Anya said. "I had to tell you before I left Shanghai."

Bia reached out and clutched Anya's hand and choked back her tears. "Thank you for risking your life to tell me this." She wiped her eyes. "When are you leaving?"

"Not sure, my prior plans got nixed by thugs."

"What?"

"Don't ask. I need to find Guy so we can get out together."

Bia scrunched her nose.

Anya held up one hand. "I know what you're going to say but this time he and I are good."

"I remember the first time he left," Bia said. "One day you're in love and life is wonderful, the next day I find you on the floor in a fetal position ready to die."

"Let's not languish in the past."

"Yeah, well, I was the one who had to put you back together."

"This time it's different."

Bia twisted her lips.

"I'm not twenty, thirty, whatever, and have learned to rule my heart where love is concerned."

Their voices went silent.

Anya twisted her finger. "I have to ask you a huge favor. I may need your help to get out of Shanghai."

Bia studied Anya, then exited the room. Anya heard indistinguishable voices in the distance. Bia returned and said, "Do you recall the place where my father had his boat moored?"

"Yes."

"We can provide you and Guy with safe passage."

She rose and embraced Bia with a tight hug. "Thank you."

"We leave in two night's time. We can't wait any longer."

"I understand." Anya pulled away. "I . . . I need a gun."

"A gun?" Bia stepped back and laughed. "You don't even know how to shoot."

"I am the daughter of a military man. While my mamma instructed me in etiquette, my papa educated me in self-defense. I'd once forgotten that, but I now know who I am."

Bia smiled. She rummaged through a cabinet until she found a tin box. She flipped open the top and withdrew a Mauser pistol. It had a long barrel and a strange wooden grip. Anya remembered her father had a similar one. He had remarked it was the best design to come out of Germany.

"It fires off ten rounds and is fully loaded." Bia handed Anya the pistol. "I must warn you. It's illegal for civilians to carry a gun. They'll kill you on sight if they find you in possession."

"I'll have to take my chances." She jammed the revolver in her coat pocket, kissed Bia on both cheeks. "I'll see you soon."

Darkness threatened to eclipse daylight when Anya departed. Soldiers now filled the streets. She could not throw off the thought of what Bia had said about getting caught with a gun. She decided to hide it for now.

Queasiness grabbed her stomach when she entered a narrow alleyway. She felt a sudden cold

shiver run through her. The further down she
walked, the more intense the feeling became. She
stopped beside a partially ravaged brick building
that held a lone bulb above a cobalt blue painted
door. She ignored the sharp pain and rummaged
through a garbage can. A foul smelly newspaper
was the only thing she found. She wrapped the
pistol in the paper and placed it underneath a pile
of old weathered wooden crates. She rinsed the
stench off her hands in a puddle of rainwater and
headed for the street. Once away from the alley the
ache in her stomach subsided. She turned around,
memorized the location, then boarded an
eastbound streetcar and headed for Guy's apartment.

She failed to notice two Japanese soldiers
several rows down as she sat on the hard wooden
bench. Her thoughts were filled with joy at having
rekindled Bia's friendship. Her attention snapped
their way when they rose from their seats. She
watched them amble towards her. Bile rose in the
back of her mouth.

The officers, dressed in black Joplin trousers
tucked inside knee high black leather boots, asked
for her papers. These men were different from the
other soldiers. Anya glanced at their holstered
weapons. Thankful, she had the forethought to hide
the revolver. She handed her papers to the lighter-

skinned man wearing round wire-rimmed glasses.

He spoke to her in English. "Where are you going?" She knew enough to ignore his inquiry. He squinted his eyes and repeated in a weak French accent.

"To visit a friend," she replied.

He looked her up and down and mumbled something to his comrade. "Come with us." The other officer with a dark olive complexion and straw-like hair that stuck out from under his cap grabbed her arm and dragged her off the streetcar.

She saw the fear in the eyes of the onlookers and struggled to free herself. "I work for the French Embassy and have diplomatic immunity. You can't treat me like this. I demand to know where you are taking me?"

"Shut up or we'll get rough with you," one of the officers shouted.

She tried to remain calm. *Guy, help me.*

TWENTY-EIGHT

ANYA FELT PERSPIRATION slide down between her shoulder blades. Two Japanese policemen had a tight grip on each of her upper arms as they marched her into a six-story modern building that resembled apartments. Several sentries with shiny bayonets attached to rifles slung over their shoulders stared as they passed by on the way to the basement. The drab cement-parking garage, now a prison, held several empty bamboo cages that looked to hold a single large dog. No bed, no chair, no blanket, only a slop bucket stuffed in the corner. The foul sour odor that filled her nostrils made her gag.

She heard the cage door creak open. The soldier with straw-like hair turned her around and put his face close to hers. His smile showed his yellow teeth. His lips tightened together then he threw her into the cell. Anya crouched alone in the cold and shivered, not sure of her next move.

Anya heard a sigh and looked across the way. There in a cage, crammed in a dark corner she saw a young girl who appeared no older than eleven. Her sullen, vacant eyes gazed in Anya's direction. She thought about Bia and how this might be her daughter, but remembered she had sent her children to the countryside. Now she knew why.

Anya endeavored to comfort the girl with a smile. The child hugged her knees to her body and turned her head away.

Images of her first arrival in Shanghai floated in her mind. She and her parents were so hopeful to start a new beginning here. Life seemed perfect before the earthquake struck, then home, family, and purpose were all lost. *Have I returned only to die in this wretched stink hole? No.* She wiped her face and nose and decided to stick with the French embassy story. Her only hope lay in Guy.

Stiff from lack of movement for what seemed hours, she struggled to stretch. But the cramped conditions did not allow her legs to unbend. There was a sudden clang of a heavy door being slammed shut. Footsteps approached. She pushed herself against the rear of her prison. The guard unlocked the cage and motioned for her to exit. She refused to move, held by fear. He grunted, stuck his arm into the pen, and yanked her out.

She uncurled herself then turned to look back at the little girl whose sunken eyes returned desperation. Her stomach coiled in a tight knot.

The soldier jabbed the butt of his rifle between her shoulder blades prodding her towards the stairs. He repeatedly hit the same sore spot. They climbed several flights before he poked her again and motioned her to enter a hallway. The well-lit passage highlighted silver-blue walls and an orange and blue patterned carpet.

He bellowed, "Stop!" in Japanese, but she continued in defiance. He yelled again. She paused and turned to a door with the painted number 666.

Anya walked into a large living room decorated in a western decor. An obese Japanese officer sat on a white davenport sipping a drink. A familiar sweet scent of cherry blossoms caused her to cough. She knew of the shadow world of sex slaves. She knew of their disdain for women. She knew what would come next.

The officer spoke in Japanese. "Who are you?"

Anya ignored his question even though she understood what he asked. The guard replied, "She doesn't speak Japanese. She's French."

The officer waved his arm about. "Interpret for me."

"I am a secretary at the French Embassy. I

work for Guy Gilot, he'll vouch for me, " she said.

The man sipped his drink then turned his attention to the interpreter. "Do you know this man?"

The guard shook his head.

The fat man laughed. "I'm sure I can make her forget about him tonight." The guard smiled and gave Anya a hungry gaze.

"You'd better wait your turn or there will be hell to pay," the guard said.

"Yeah, yeah." The officer struggled to pull himself off the davenport and drunkenly staggered towards her. Anya's heart pounded.

His knuckles stroked her cheek. "Nice." Her facial muscles tightened. He palmed the pendent that hung around her neck. Her back stiffened. He walked behind her and placed his hands on her shoulders then slowly ran them down her arms. Her skin prickled.

She felt like a cornered mouse. Her instincts told her that if she moved it would give the wolf motive to pounce. She felt his hot breath on the nape of her neck and suppressed the vomit that rose in her throat.

A knock at the door forced the men's attention away from her. Behind, she heard a man mumble something, then the door closed. She turned around to find herself alone. A breath exploded from her chest and she collapsed in a chair. She swabbed her eyes, took a deep breath, then squeezed the pendant in her hand. "No matter what happens, I must stay alive."

Anya heard the doorknob turn. She jumped up and stood rigid. A soldier, taller than the others, with rounder eyes, entered the room. He wore a different uniform with epaulets on the shoulders. She tried to swallow but her mouth was as dry as the Gobi.

If I try to put myself somewhere pleasant, it will be over soon. She remembered a time, as a child, when she and her parents traveled by train across Siberia on their way to a new town and a new adventure. Along the route, the train had engine trouble and had to stop for repairs. They disembarked and walked together alongside a lush pink-carpeted meadow that led to a large clear green-blue lake. In the distance, the mountain caps still held winter's snow. A perfume of wild flowers permeated the air. Life could not have been sweeter.

Anya felt the nudge of a hand against the small of her back. She became confused when he pushed her out of the room. He escorted her to a waiting elevator then shoved her in. He remained outside the elevator while he reached around and pushed the button for the lobby. Opaque black vacant eyes stared at her as the doors shut.

She watched the metal arrow move from 10 to 9 to 8 . . . Her mind raced to the possibility of the doors opening with guns pointed ready to shoot her dead. Her breathing became heavy by the time she reached the lobby. The doors opened and there, instead of guns, was Guy.

She ran into his arms, buried her head in his chest, and cried out. "Get me out of here."

"Do you still have it?" he whispered.

Her face still hidden, she nodded.

"Good, let's go." He unlocked her tight embrace and guided her through the front door. Two guards with drawn weapons and a grim expression watched their every move.

Halfway down the street Anya stopped to say something. Guy interrupted, "Keep walking, they're watching us." They reached the car and Guy opened the door for her. "Quick, get in before they change their minds and shoot us."

He started the engine with his eyes glued on the guards standing out front. "Show me."

Anya lifted the locket from under her blouse. "How did you know where to find me?"

Guy put the car in gear and drove off. "Your communist friends saw you get picked up by the Kempeitai. Do you know the Kempeitai?"

Anya shrugged her shoulders and shook her head.

"Secret Police, the SS of the Japanese army. I know the commandant. I reminded him he owed me a favor. That, and a bribe goes a long way in this town." He glanced over in her direction. "You are one lucky little lady."

"I know." She wrenched down on her finger.

He hesitated then blurted out, "Shelley's dead."

"I know, Joe and Mac told me."

"Really, that's very interesting." Guy strummed his fingers on the steering wheel. "When you didn't show up I got worried and went to see Shelley. I found his body slumped in his chair with his head resting on his desk. Didn't appear he'd been tortured, no distinguished marks on his wrists or neck. They may have forced him to ingest something to make it look like suicide."

"You suspect—Joe?"

"Not sure, although, I spotted him when I was tailing Mac."

"I don't believe it. He loved Shelley."

"Everyone will one day pry your fingers from their raft and watch you drown. It's the way of the world."

"Joe did hand me over to gangsters." Anya crossed her arms.

"Look kiddo, things are getting complicated." Guy pulled alongside the curb and shut off the car's engine.

"Where are we?" she said.

"Nowhere, I need to tell you something. I saw Mac get into a black sedan and I don't imagine they were going sightseeing.

"Jesus, Green Gang?"

"That'd be my guess."

Anya sat motionless. "We have to help him."

"Are you crazy, these guys are ruthless. You don't mess with these people."

"There can't be more than two. I shoot one. You shoot the other."

Guy exhaled then snickered, "This isn't the movies. The good guys don't always get the bad guys." He shook his head still laughing. "You've been in America too long."

"He needs our help." Anya's voice took on a high pitch.

"I thought you hated the guy."

"I've been unfair where Mac is concerned." She bit her bottom lip. "His dedication and loyalty to his assignment has been admirable. He reminds me of my papa." She sighed and hung her head. "I've been tenacious, tumultuous and plain troublesome. I've put this mission in jeopardy and placed him in harm's way. I may be the cause of Mac's abduction."

"I seriously doubt it. He seems the type that finds trouble."

She lifted her head and faced Guy. "Please do this. It's important to me."

"Okay. But first we need to find that little bitch."

TWENTY-NINE

D USK BLANKETED THE skyline as a hard rain fell on the windshield of Guy's Peugeot. "Why are we sitting here? Let's just go in and get him," Anya said.

"I don't go into a place where I don't know how to get out. Be patient," Guy said.

"This is worse than waiting for Christmas morning." She banged her head on the back of the car seat.

Guy smiled but kept his eyes on the teashop. "He is going to need you after this."

Anya turned to Guy. "What are you talking about?"

"Your American friend. He's alone in a foreign country with no contacts. He's going to need to rely on you." He tapped his fingers on the steering wheel. "But, I think you know that."

"What are you insinuating?"

"If you're willing to risk both our lives to rescue him, there's more to him then you admit."

She crossed her arms over her chest. "I'm not in love with Mac, if that's what you think."

Guy remained stationary with one eyebrow crooked.

Anya stared out the side window. *Why has my relationship with Mac been so turbulent? Maybe I've been too judgmental and quick-tempered with him. He's just so damn . . .*

"There." Guy pointed. "That's the little punk. Stay here while I get him."

Guy jumped out, pulled the collar of his trench coat up, and walked across the street. Anya saw Joe jump when Guy grabbed him. Joe squirmed to untangle himself as Guy muscled him across the street. The sedan back door opened and Guy shoved Joe in then climbed in beside him.

"Slide over Anya, and drive," Guy said.

"What's going on? Where you take me?" Joe screamed as the car drove off.

Anya felt the car rock as Joe tried to wrestle with the door handle.

"Calm down little man," Guy wiped rainwater from his face. "We just want to have a chat."

"What about?" Joe's teeth chattered.

In the rearview mirror Anya watched Joe's eyes

dart to her then Guy.

Guy said, "We want to know where Yu-seng has taken Mac."

"Search me?" Joe's bloodless lips trembled.

"Stop with the Hardy Boys lingo. Besides me, you were the last person to see him step into Yu-seng's car. Don't deny it, I saw you. And if my assumptions are right, you had something to do with it."

"I know nothing."

Guy backhanded Joe across the face. Joe cried out. Anya cringed and glanced at Joe in the mirror. She pulled down an alley and stopped the car.

"Don't waste my time. Where have they taken him?" Guy raised his fist.

Joe whimpered as tears fell from his swollen red cheek.

"Hang on, Guy." Anya turned around, her chin rested on the back of the seat. In a soft melodic tone she said, "I'm sorry Joe, this is important, we need answers. Did you murder Shelley?"

"No. I love him. I never hurt him. Honest, I not know they kill Shelley. I found him dead at desk. Mr. Shelley try to help me.

"I know you'd never intentionally hurt Shelley, but why Mac?" Anya said.

"They say they kill Uncle if I no help. He take me in. I owe him utmost loyalty. They say I tell about you and Mr. Mac or they kill me."

Guy clutched Joe's shirt collar. "Who tried to do away with me?"

Joe shrugged. "Maybe, new guy."

"Who? What does he look like?" Guy said.

"He not Chinese. He look like Mongolian peasant."

"Sun." Guy looked at Anya. "God. Can this get any more convoluted?"

"Joe, think," Anya said. "What did you tell them about Mac and me?"

Joe continued to whimper, "I only say where you go, who you meet. That all." Joe wiped his nose on his shirtsleeve. "I not know what Mr. Shelley tell Yu-seng."

"Enough," Guy said. "Let's kill him."

Anya eyed Guy. "Stop with the death threats." She lowered her voice. "It's okay, Joe. Just tell us where Mac is."

"They took him to empty warehouse at shipping lanes. Last pier."

"You damn well better be telling the truth or I'll be back." Guy opened the door and kicked Joe out. "They'll know you've spoken with us and will come looking for you. Best if you and your uncle get out of town."

Anya sped away. From the review mirror, she saw Joe, soaked and sobbing in the rain.

THIRTY

Mac REGAINED CONSCIOUSNESS to find himself, strung up and stripped naked with both arms secured behind his back. His torso hung forward and his toes just touched the ground. The damp cold air penetrated to his marrow. He knew in a second where he was—an empty building, the perfect place to grill someone.

Sun smack a rubber hose against his palm. Mac's training told him that he would only be able to endure for so long before he would reveal everything.

"We know you're a spy. What we want to know is why you are in China?" Sun said.

Mac wheezed. "I'm a French importer looking to export high quality opium."

"Our sources tell us differently." Sun took the tube and swung it with all his might, striking Mac's groin. Mac raised his head and howled, then vomited. Blood leaked beneath the rope that held his biceps.

"You don't scream like a Frenchman," Sun laughed. "In fact, you shriek like an American."

"Who are your sources?" Mac used his mind to push the pain away and tried to catch his breath. "Maybe I can clarify the misunderstanding."

Sun chuckled. "We are not fools. Interrogation has been a part of our culture for centuries. We've had time to perfect it."

"Nice to know." Mac felt the smack of something hard against his cheekbone. An upper molar loosened. It held a metallic taste in his mouth similar to a tarnished nickel.

"I won't ask you again." Sun said. "Why are you in China?"

Mac dislodged the wobbly tooth with his tongue and spit it at Sun. The molar bounced off Sun's flat nose.

Another blow between his legs caused Mac to yowl, a flash of his wife and daughter filled his mind before he passed out.

IT WAS LATE afternoon by the time Anya found the alley where she had stashed the Mauser. She stopped and turned to Guy. "This place gives me the creeps. I can't explain it, but it's like someone is squeezing my chest making it hard to breath."

"Stay here. I'll get it. Where did you hide the gun?"

"Under a stack of crates—over there—by the blue door."

Guy lifted the top crate, then a second one and searched around. "I can't find it."

"It has to be there." She pushed through her trepidation and rushed over to Guy. "I can't understand it. I placed it right here."

A moan from the other side of the alley caused them both to turn. Crumpled in a corner was a man in tattered clothing, propped up against the side of a building. He coughed and wiped his nose on his filthy sleeve.

Guy approached with caution. He saw the pistol on the man's lap. The man's blackened face left only the whites of his eyes identifiable. He picked up the gun, his hand rested on his lap and pointed it at Guy.

Guy held up his hands and took a step back. "We're not here to hurt you. We only want the gun."

The man remained motionless. Guy slowly moved forward with the gun still aimed at him. He was within a few feet when he noticed the man was bleeding. "I think he's been shot."

Anya rushed over. Guy held up his hand to stop her. He bent down and felt the man's neck for a pulse. "I think he's dead." He removed the gun from the man's hand.

"What should we do?"

"Nothing we can do." Guy closed the man's eyes. "Let's go."

THE RAIN HAD stopped and the clouds cleared to expose a gibbous moon anchored high in the sky when Anya and Guy arrived at the abandoned warehouse. They crept in through a side door and stood for a moment. Faint moonlight shone in from loft windows as their eyes adjusted. The lower floor was empty. A few broken light fixtures with exposed electrical wires hung overhead. A section of the corner backend of the building had been bombed out rendering additional light. On opposite sides, two stairways rose to a second level alcove.

"Listen, I hear noises coming from above," Anya said.

"Go up these stairs. I'll go to the other side of the building and come up from behind. That way we can cut off their escape," Guy said.

Anya nodded. She tightened her grip on the Mauser pistol and crept up the stairs. Beads of perspiration dotted her brow, as she climbed. Her breath grew heavier with each step. The noises became voices when she reached the top.

"Throw some water on him and wake him up. I think he has more to tell us," a man said.

"Sun said to wait until he returned."

Anya pressed forward with trepidation. Her foot touched a rickety floorboard. A screech resonated down the hallway. Frozen in place, the grip on the gun fell loose against her wet palm. She readjusted her grasp and waited for one of the gangsters to investigate. Footsteps neared, but no one emerged. She continued then halted at a partition with small paned glass windows on the upper half. The glass held years of dirt, making it difficult to see through.

Anya found a clean streak and spotted Mac hanging unconscious. She covered her mouth. *God, please let him be alive.*

Two men paced around Mac. The larger of the two spoke, "Where is Sun? He should've been back by now. I'm hungry." Anya recognized one of the men. He had tried to kidnap her at the teahouse. Her neck hairs bristled and she felt her finger tighten around the trigger.

Anya spotted Guy across the room. He nodded to her then advanced. He aimed his pistol at the larger thug. "Good evening, gentlemen."

Both men went for their guns.

"Hold on boys. We don't want a fight. We're only here to pick up our friend," Guy said.

The smaller thug, not much taller than Anya, raised his gun at Guy. Anya stepped into the room. "Not so fast, small fry," she said. "I don't want to shoot you and you don't want to be dead. And at this range I can't miss."

Anya heard his barrel recoil and she fired. The bullet pierced the man's hand, forcing him to drop his firearm. The larger man fired off a couple of shots at Guy. Guy returned fire then dove behind a stack of wooden crates.

She whipsawed her attention to Guy then darted over to the small man who was going for his gun. She leaped at him, knocking him down. Out of the corner of her eye, she saw a gun pointed in her direction from across the room. She rolled the little man on top of her. Two shots hit him in the back and his body went limp.

Guy ran out and pistol-whipped the gunman on the head, knocking him down and comatose.

"Are you all right?" Guy said.

"Yeah, get this cretin off me."

Guy dragged the corpse off Anya then helped her up. He untied Mac, who collapsed to the ground. He gave Anya a quizzical look. "What?"

"You're shot," Anya shouted. Blood streamed down Guy's arm.

Guy examined the back of his upper arm. "It's just a flesh wound, I'll be okay."

Anya studied Mac's naked body lying in a fetal position. "We can't take him like that."

Guy rubbed his chin then snapped his fingers. He stripped the unconscious man of his clothes and dressed Mac. Then he hoisted him over his shoulder like a sack of russets. "Let's go," he said.

They hurried down the stairs and out the door to the car.

Guy shoved Mac into the backseat of the sedan while Anya dashed around to the driver's side. A shot from several yards away ricocheted off the ground in front of Anya.

"Anya, go—now," Guy ordered.

Anya jumped in and started up the engine as Guy slid in next to Mac. She gunned it, spinning the tires on rocks. Dirt, dust, and debris flew into the air. Guy returned fire from the passenger window as they sped away.

"Who the hell is that?" Anya said.

"Sun," Guy said.

Several shots crashed through the back window.

Anya looked in the rearview mirror. Mac remained unconscious. She glanced at Guy, his body slumped in the backseat, blood flowed from a hole in his neck.

THIRTY-ONE

OCEAN WAVES CRASHED down on top of Anya. She tried to keep her head above water but with each breath, water filled her lungs. Panic swelled with each cough. View-Master images of her mother and father, of Pete, Paval, and Guy flashed by. She heard a strange voice from behind call to her. She turned to see who beckoned. A hard wave broadsided and tossed her under. Caught in its undertow, she swam hard. The force of the water rolled her over and over and over. The pressure in her lungs became excruciating, her arms and legs became numb. She faded in and out of consciousness Her body released a sudden jerk and she drew in a deep breath. She opened her eyes, gulped in a mouthful of air, and found herself crumpled in a chair.

Dawn peeked through the curtain slit as she

wiped the cool stickiness of the nightmare's sweat from her brow.

Mac lay in bed. His breath was labored. He bore deep gashes in his arms where the rope had sliced into his flesh. One side of his swollen face displayed red blotches surrounded by blue-purple bruising.

Anya picked up the tin of balm from the nightstand and applied it to his wounds. His skin felt as cold as the dead. He moaned and thrashed his arms about. She jumped back to escape a blow to her jaw.

Mac yelled out, "Cora—Cora."

She grabbed his arms and struggled to push them down. "Mac, it's Anya. You're safe."

Mac cracked open his eyes. His once mischievous blue eyes now held a dull cast. Not quite conscious, his eyes darted around with the wildness of an injured animal.

"It's Anya," she repeated. "Can you hear me?"

He relaxed and nodded. A moment later, he murmured. "How did you find me?"

"We paid a visit to a mutual friend," she said with raised eyebrows.

His eyes opened. "That weasel. Wait till I get my hands on him." He winced and he fought to sit up but his head fell onto the pillow.

"You have quite a shiner. How many fingers am

I holding up?"

"Two."

"Just checking for head trauma. I'll get some ice for your face." She shouted from the kitchen. "I'm sure Joe and his Uncle have moved on by now. It's not going to be safe for them in Shanghai." She returned and placed a compress on Mac's cheek.

"How do you feel?" she said.

"Like someone beat the crap out of me."

"I see you haven't lost your sense of humor." She sat in a chair next to the bed.

"Where am I?" Fully conscious, he scanned the room. "I don't recognize this place."

She hesitated. "Guy's apartment."

"Where is he?"

Anya lowered her head and fidgeted with her finger. She stuttered, "He, he didn't make it." She brushed a tear from her lashes.

"I'm sorry, Anya," Mac laid his hand on her forearm and squeezed. "I'm sorry. I . . . ah, he was a good man."

She fell back in the chair and looked out the window. The sun had totally risen. She fondled the snakehead necklace. Her body ached but she refused to cry. Fragmented images of Guy filled her mind. She remembered the tenderness of his hand across her face. The pungent sandalwood cologne he wore. The gentle whispers in her ear as they

252 • P. C. CHINICK

made love.

"Seems, I'm bad luck where men are concerned."

"I'm still with you."

Anya tilted her head. "Parts of you anyway." She held a half smile.

He pulled the bedding off and groaned. His body trembled when he lowered one leg to the floor then the other.

"Where do you think you're going?" she said.

"I have to . . ." He coughed in his fist.

Anya grabbed his legs, placed them back on the bed, and covered him. "Oh, no you don't. You're under my orders now and you require rest."

"Yes, ma'am," he muttered and closed his eyes.

She laid the cool cloth on his forehead and gazed upon his face. *Men always have an angelic expression when they're asleep.*

THE TWO O'CLOCK chimes from the clock on the mantel woke Anya. She heard Mac cry out from the other room and went to investigate.

Mac flailed underneath the sheets. He screamed out "Stop. Cora—wait." He sat up wide-eyed and breathless.

"Who's Cora?" Anya straightened the bedding.

Mac eyes shot away. "What?"

"You keep shouting for someone named Cora."

He squirmed beneath the sheets. "No one."

"It might help pacify your dreams if you talk about it." Anya jammed her hands on her hips.

"You're not going to leave me alone until I tell you, are you?"

"Nope."

He heaved a sigh. "You may not relish what you hear."

"I'll take my chances." She settled in the chair and crossed her ankles.

Mac sat up, leaned on the headboard, and tucked the blanket around his waist. He cleared his throat. "You recall I told you, I killed a woman?"

Anya nodded.

"I worked for MI-5 in London during the blitz. My job entailed passing false information to German intelligence. My contact was a stout man who donned a tan Burberry trench coat and carried a brown umbrella even when the sun was out.

"We devised an exchange scenario. I would raise my coat collar round my neck, bend down, and tie my shoe to signal a pass. Then reach inside my coat pocket, pull out a crumpled scrap of paper, and drop it on the ground. He would pass, stab the paper with the point of his umbrella, and continue down the path. It sounds clumsy but the handoff always worked."

"I'll have to pay better attention to people in the future," she said.

"After I returned home that day, I heard noises from inside my flat. I kicked in the door in an attempt to knock over the intruder. A surprised Cora stood there with eyes the size of billiard balls. She too was a spy, under orders from Germany. I'd been seeing her for several months. I'd used her to infiltrate a network of Nazis living in London."

"Did you get much information from her?" she said.

Mac pursed his lips then continued. "I noticed her cheek flushed when I kissed it. I asked her why she'd come. She stammered and paced about saying we had scheduled lunch together. I knew something was wrong but became preoccupied with having to send a transmission to headquarters and ignored my instincts. I told her to go ahead and I'd meet her at the restaurant.

"After she left, I opened the wardrobe where I stashed my gear. I instantly saw I'd been compromised. My shirts and trousers were jammed to one side and a rear panel where I hid the transmitter was ajar. I wrenched off the backboards and found the device smashed.

"My heart pounded faster than a rabbit running for its life. My mind immediately raced to Cora. I dashed to the apartment hallway and peered down the stairwell. I saw her take the first step onto the lobby floor.

"I hollered after her that I'd changed my mind and we should go together. She looked up, squinted at me, and ran."

Mac reached for the glass of water on the night stand and took a sip. Anya sat forward waiting for him to continue.

"I rushed down the stairs three at a time. Outside the building, I spotted her turn the corner. I raced ahead and spied her again, trying to blend into the crowd. I tried to conceal myself, but I tend to tower over most people. She turned around, saw me, and took off. Then made her way to the Underground. By the time I'd reached the tunnel, I wasn't sure which direction she'd gone. I chose to go left and ended up on a platform where only a woman and small child sat on a bench. I sped back to the other passageway as the train pulled up. I caught sight of her at the end of the platform. She, in turn, saw me. I climbed on board a few cars away when she did. I knew enough to stay near the door. When the doors closed, she jumped off. I suspected she would. I jammed my body between the doors and grappled to yank them apart.

"She had to run by me to escape. Still caught in the train door, I grabbed a piece of her coat. She slipped her arms out and raced up the tunnel then above ground. I finally reached the top and caught a glimpse of her scurrying down an alley. My adrenaline sped into overdrive to catch her. I reached the alley to see her in a frantic attempt to open locked doors. Her eyes zipped around for a way out."

Anya empathized with how Cora must have felt. She experienced the same terror during her arrest by the Japanese Kempeitai.

"I sought to calm her," Mac said. "Explaining I wanted to talk. She shrieked at me in German, calling me a bastard, a degenerate, a traitor. I reassured her that I wasn't going to hurt her. She spat at me and called me a liar. I told her that's what spies do."

"Not a smart thing to say," Anya said.

"No kidding. She came at me with her nails flared. I grabbed her wrists and twisted her around so her back pressed against my chest then held her until she gave in. Once she quieted, I crooked my arm around her neck and clamped it tight against her carotid artery until she lost consciousness, then snapped her neck.

"How did that make you feel?"

Mac's eye darted from her and lowered his head. "They prepare you for a lot of situations, but killing someone with your bare hands is something that will haunt you."

Anya sat still in her chair, her hands folded. She recollected what Edmund Atwater had said to her about Mac being her lifeline. *The loneliest place is when you have no one to trust.*

She looked into Mac's one good eye. "Spies don't play the same social rules." She twisted her finger. "I want to apologize for my behavior. I understand who you are now. I didn't know that a few days ago. I only knew that I despised you. I misjudged you, I'm sorry."

Mac smiled. "I kinda liked how you didn't fall all over me unlike most women." His face turned rosy. "Although, it did made it harder to direct you."

"If I have learned anything in these last few days, it's that when forced, we must go against social convention to save this bloody world from its own ignorance." Mac's nod indicated for the first time that they were in lockstep.

Mac lifted the blanket up to see white skivvies. "Who undressed me?"

"The better question is who dressed me?"

"What?"

She turned away. "Forget it."

Mac smiled, wrapped himself with the blanket, then clambered out of bed. "I need to get to the consulate."

"In all seriousness, your face looks similar to a

Picasso with a couple of pieces missing and from the bruises on your side, I'm sure you have one or two cracked ribs."

"I must complete my mission." He grimaced in pain while he rummaged through Guy's dresser. He removed the top drawer and dumped the contents on the bed.

"What are you looking for?" she said.

"Spies hide guns like misers stash money." Mac extracted the middle drawer. He noticed it was shorter than the other one. He flipped it around to see a Smith & Wesson .38 Special along with a silencer taped to the back of the drawer. He untapped the two then checked the gun chambers to find it fully loaded then slapped the cylinder back into place.

Anya remained seated. "I know anything I say will go unheeded but . . ."

He jerked the top sheet then tore it into strips.

"What are you doing?" she said.

Mac fumbled with a cloth band trying to wrap his ribcage.

"Here, let me do it."

He rested his hand on her shoulder while she secured a tight fit.

"Can you walk?"

"I'll be fine," he said.

"You'll want some clean clothes." She removed

a shirt and pair of trousers from Guy's closet.

Mac rolled up the shirtsleeves and cinched the belt beyond the usual worn marks.

Anya sucked in air at the sight of Mac in Guy's clothes. "Sorry, it's just . . ."

Mac walked into the bathroom, splashed cold water on his unshaven face, and stared at his image in the mirror. "Anya, I gave you little consequence." He turned to her and patted his face dry with a towel. "It's not easy for me to say please, but I need your help."

Anya stared at him. "I think we both need each other."

THIRTY-TWO

THEY ARRIVED AT the consulate through the tunnels and headed for Shelley's office. Anya stopped short of the office when she thought she heard something upstairs. She turned to listen but deemed it was nothing and caught up with Mac.

Anya stared at the vacant desk. She remembered that last time she saw Shelley.

"You look puzzled. What's the matter," Mac said.

"I just assumed Shelley's body would still be here."

"Someone's come for it."

"Joe," they said in unison.

Mac made his way to the desk.

"What are we looking for?" Anya said.

"I'll know it when I find it," he replied.

She mumbled, "It might be nice to have some

kind of idea so I could help."

"I think Shelley might have been passing on information to Yu-seng," Mac said. "Maybe the letter of introduction he gave me to give to Yu-seng wasn't an introduction but a disclosure. I believe that underneath that cherub Santa façade lay a cunning man whose loyalties only went as far as the Chinese."

Mac sat behind the desk and passed his hand over the wood grain. He pulled open the top drawer to find pencils, pens, and a notebook. He flipped through the pages of the empty book then put it back. He opened the side drawers to discover the multitude of files gone. His eyes darted back to the top drawer. He removed the notebook and rubbed his finger over the first blank page.

He took a lead pencil and scratched the surface of the paper. "Got something." A faint white outline appeared in the graphite:

NS - OF - 11

Anya peered over his shoulder. "What does it mean?"

Mac studied the script. "Don't know, but the handwriting is the same as the note I received." He frowned. "Do you know of a place with the initials N.S.?" He ran his fingers through his hair.

Anya chewed an index fingernail. "NS. NS. NS. Um, ah, ah . . .north south—north section—

North Station . . . "

"What's North Station?" he interrupted.

"It's a train station on the other side of the river."

"That's it." Mac snapped his fingers. "North Station at 11 o'clock. It all fits. I received a message earlier, at the hotel when you and Joe were in the other room. It mentioned Li was in town."

"I thought that was a ruse to get you out of the hotel," Anya said.

"They were banking on the fact I'd be dead, so why not tell the truth."

"Why would Shelley have this information?"

"Either he's been working with them or against them. Maybe that's why they killed him." Mac folded the paper and placed it in his pocket.

"Maybe Shelley tried to help you," Anya said.

"We'll never know the truth."

Anya picked up the paper. "What does OF mean?"

"You tell me. You're the expert at decipher."

"Yeah, when I have a codebook."

They were about to leave when they heard voices coming from the foyer.

Anya's eyes darted over to Mac.

"What are they saying?" Mac whispered.

"I can't make it out. It sounds like there are only two of them."

The clack, clack, clack, on the marble floor grew louder as they passed the office.

An uncontrollable hunger hiccup escaped from Anya. She slapped her hand to her mouth to smother the sound, but it was too late. The footsteps stopped.

A tall gangly Chinese man entered the room, while the other waited inside the doorway. Mac positioned himself between the bookcase and behind the office door while Anya sat at the desk.

The beady black-eyed man stared her down. "How did you get in here?"

"Through the front door." She smiled.

Mac braced himself against the bookcase then raised one leg and kicked the door hitting the man in the entryway hard enough to knock him out.

The other man's quick reflexes had his foot in the air catching Mac on the chin. Before Mac could react, he was on the ground. The man lifted his foot to smash Mac's face. Mac grabbed it and twisted until it cracked. The man bellowed and turned into the twist. Mac kicked the man's feet out from under him. Both were on the floor, wrapped in each other's arms, like Greco-Roman wrestlers.

Mac gasped for breath as the thug's hands tightened around his throat. There was a crash and then the man collapsed.

Anya stood over them, holding part of a

RED ASSCHER • 265

Chinese vase. The remains lay shattered on the ground. "I figured you could take him but I wasn't in the mood to wait around." She winked.

"Thanks." Mac slowly hoisted himself off the ground.

"Who are they?"

"Green Gang members, no doubt." He stood and brushed himself off.

"What do you think they were doing here?"

"Who knows? Pilfering most likely. In any case, we need to get out before they come around. How do we get to the North Station?"

"The tunnels don't extend that far. We'll have to travel above ground once we reach the river."

Mac said, "Let's mount up."

THIRTY-THREE

T HE STENCH OF the tunnel and Mac's shortness of breath made him cough. He grabbed his side.

"Are you all right?" Anya said.

"This bent position puts pressure on my ribs. Once we get out of here I'll be fine."

They climbed up the iron ladder and left the safety of the tunnels. Together they snaked along dark passageways mindful of patrols. Anya stopped before venturing over the footbridge. On the other side of the river a Japanese soldier lit a cigarette. His face glowed in the flame of the match.

"Is there another way across?" Mac whispered.

"It's a ways up Suzhou Creek, but I'm sure it'll be guarded."

They watched the sentry walk down the street. Mac's heel caught a loose stone as the guard moved on. The sound attracted the soldier's attention. He turned around. They held their breaths when he marched towards them.

An emaciated orange striped cat strolled by Anya into the light and yowled. The soldier muttered something then lifted his rifle and shot at the cat. Screeches echoed in the night as the cat flailed about on the roadway. Anya covered her mouth to stifle a scream and squeezed her eyes shut. Mac placed a comforting hand on her shoulder. A second shot silenced the cat's agony. The soldier then walked away. They waited for him to step out of view before they emerged from the darkness.

"Everything okay?" Mac said.

Anya wiped her eyes and nose, and nodded.

The footbridge spanned a narrow point in the creek at about twenty paces across. Along the bank, several sampans lay anchored, piled high with produce ready for the next day's market. They felt the eyes of silent boatmen follow them as they crossed over the bridge and crept into the heavily guarded section of the city.

"Joe warned me this part of town is dangerous," Mac said as they walked down a darkened alley.

Anya stopped. "We can always go back."

Mac shook his head. "Out of the question."

A loud rumble froze them in their footsteps just

as they were about to exit the alley. Their eyes locked on each other. The ground shook under their feet and the noise grew louder. Braced against a brick building they waited. A two-man tank sped by followed by a truckload of Japanese troops.

Mac's chestnut hair blew straight up from the wake of wind left behind. "That was close."

"It's just a little further," Anya said.

She took the lead, continued across the street and down a few more alleys. Anya pointed at a partially crumbled building several yards ahead. "That's North Station," she paused. "What's left of it."

The once three-story building all but lay in rubble. Two connecting sides remained upright. A few lights glowed in the distance

They plodded through an open field with ankle high grass to the station. Anya could hear Mac's heavy breathing. "Are you all right?"

"Can you tighten these bandages?"

Collected, they ventured on to the terminal entrance. Anya jumped when a Chinese man dressed in a western style suit ran by them.

"Don't look so nervous." Mac took Anya's arm and walked her under what remained of an arched doorway. "We're just a couple traveling, nothing unusual about that."

"Are you kidding?" she said.

"If you look like you know what you're doing, usually no one will take notice. We'll just blend in."

"With your height and my red hair, yeah, we blend–like oil and vinegar."

Mac nudged Anya down an isolated and dim corridor that led to an empty platform. He placed his hand in front to stop her. They remained silent in the shadows.

One large pillar was all that remained on the cement landing. The roof was all but gone allowing the near full moon to light the surface. At the end, where trains at one time entered and exited, lay a dark abyss. The place was void of people and trains.

"Where's the train?" Anya whispered.

"Not sure."

From around the pillar a man strutted away, towards the darkness. He wore a black coat and fedora, and twirled a cane.

"Who's the weird little fellow?" Anya said.

Mac replied, "Sun."

The hair on the back of Anya's neck bristled. She had a mind to pull out her gun and shoot him dead. *No, that would be too easy. A bullet in the belly is what he deserves for killing Guy.*

"I thought we were looking for Li," Anya said.

"Sun's our connection."

She liked his use of the term our. It made her feel a genuine part of the mission. However, her pride washed away when she glanced back at Sun. Vengeance now consumed her.

Mac pulled out the Smith & Wesson and attached the silencer.

Anya inched forward but Mac took her wrist. "Stay put. I'll signal when I need you. And for God's sake, don't shoot unless absolutely necessary. We can't afford to have the Japanese Army on us."

"Don't be such a worrywart."

MAC APPEARED OUT from the tunnel with his coat draped over his arm, hiding the gun. His eyes darted around.

Sun faced Mac. "Did you enjoy the beating so much you're back for more?"

"I'd like to say I missed your ugly mug, but I'm here looking for Dai Li."

"I am sorry to disappoint you, but he's not here." Sun continued to twirl his cane.

"You don't mind if I take a look." Mac revealed his gun and pointed it at Sun's chest.

Sun slowly put his hands in the air. "Help yourself."

Mac relieved the cane from Sun's grip. "I'm going to ask you once more. Where is Li?"

Sun's eyes flashed towards the end of the platform. Beyond the ramp lay an open field. Several yards out, Mac could just make out the silhouette of an engine.

He looked down at the tracks. From the top of the ledge, it looked like a six-foot drop. He motioned Sun to the edge then pushed him over. Sun fell on his side with a howl. Mac hit the ground with a moan and held his ribs. He shook it off and jammed the gun into Sun's back. "Let's take a walk," he said through his teeth.

Convenient clouds masked the moonlight as Mac repeatedly poked Sun in the back with the butt of the cane. They hiked along the rails then came upon a metal gray engine and two cars resting on abandoned tracks. Concerned he might have failed crossed his mind, then he spotted a deep scratch that exposed dark green paint. He knew this was the right train, the one used by Nationalist dignitaries to move about the country.

"I'm telling you . . ." Sun said.

"Shut your pie hole and hop on," Mac said.

They boarded the unlit sleeping car. The clouds had passed and moonlight shown through the windows that stretched the length of the train. Mac instructed Sun to slide open the first door to one of the private compartments then shoved him aside while he inspected inside. He reached his hand inside and flipped on the light switch. The dark paneled room had a patterned padded bench seat with one chair in the opposite corner and a table below the window.

"I told you, no Li," Sun said.

Mac gestured for Sun to march ahead to the second compartment. Sun stepped backwards with a broad smile. A face reflected off the train window alerted Mac that someone was behind him. Before he had time to turn around, Mac felt a sharp blow at the nape of his neck.

ANYA DID NOT wait for Mac's signal. When she saw him jump off the platform, she quickly followed, keeping a good distance behind. She clutched the pistol, finger on the trigger, and crept up the metal steps onto the train car. The end of a cabin wall hid her from sight. She poked her head around the corner to see Mac lying in the corridor. *God, can't that guy stay on his feet.* She slinked out of sight to gather her thoughts. *What do I do? What do I do? What do I do?*

Images of Guy slumped in the back car seat and Mac strung up by his arms made her grit her teeth. She steadied her nerves and with gun in hand, tiptoed down the hall.

Sun's lackey stepped out into the hall and froze. Anya motioned for him to return inside. She heard Sun yell, "What are you waiting for?"

Anya moved in front of the doorway with Mac at her feet, his gun next to him, her gun pointed at Sun.

"And who have we here?" Sun licked his lips.

The gun trembled in her hands.

Sun said, "Drop it honey. You don't know how to use it."

Anya's back stiffened and she fixed her aim. "Didn't anyone ever tell you not to antagonize someone with a weapon?" She fired a shot, nicking Sun's ear. He jumped, grabbed the side of his face. A small trace of blood stained his fingers.

"Guess I'm a bit rusty," she shrugged. "I was going for the entire ear."

Anya ordered the other man to lock himself in the bathroom. He obeyed her without hesitation.

"Let's you and I have a talk. Take a seat," she said.

Anya saw a touch of evil around Sun's mouth and eyes. She stared at him with all the hatred she could muster. The gun poised, ready to slice open his gut.

THIRTY-FOUR

MAC REMAINED OUT cold on the floor. Anya knelt with the gun on Sun and felt Mac's neck for a pulse. She was relieved he was still alive. She picked up the Smith & Wesson that lay next to him. The .38 felt more comfortable in her hand. She sat in the chair across from Sun and placed the Mauser behind her back.

Sun sat back in his seat with his legs stretched forward.

"Comfortable?" Anya said.

He smiled. She squeezed the butt of the gun while her finger twitched on the trigger. She imagined pulling it and then bits of his brain splattering against the wall.

His bangs fell askew across his forehead, exposing a deep hairline scar. "Looks like someone tried to scalp you."

He ignored her.

She wondered if the assailant who marked him got away.

A fly buzzed around the room and landed on his nose. Sun swatted at it several times. "Flies are attracted to decaying rotting matter." She smiled.

"Don't forget you're in the room too." Sun tried to smash it but the fly managed to get away.

"It's all about killing with you." She chewed on her words. "You really are a monster, the kind who exists to murder. Or do you refer to it as elimination?"

Sun retained a casual posture with crossed legs and unfolded arms while his face held a smirk. His cane rested next to him.

Anya continued, "You hunt your prey, find them and make sure they know your intent before you strike."

Sun squinted. "Ah, the smell of fear. It has a pungent odor. Something I've come to enjoy." He chuckled. "It's not the kill, it's the terror. Tell me my dear, what scares you?"

Beads of cold sweat formed at her temples. She stuck out her chin and glared. "Is that what you did to Shelley? Frightened him?"

"Ha, the fat old fag." Sun crossed his arms tight against his chest. "He thought himself Chinese, but he was just another white, sharp-nosed infidel.

Maybe he dropped dead from the stress of betraying his own people."

Anya frowned. "What are you talking about?"

"He funneled secret information to the Nationalists and worked with the Green Gang. How do you think we knew about the two of you?"

"You're lying." She waved the gun at him.

"Believe what you want."

Anya glanced over at Mac's crumpled body. "Did you inject him with something?"

"You interrupted me." Sun grinned.

The fly beat against the cabin window. Anya desperately wanted to open the window so they could all escape.

"Your friend, the Frenchman, he was a challenge," Sun said.

Anya sat up, her eyes narrowed. "What?"

"At the tearoom. You two looked so intimate, so cozy, so in love. I'm almost sorry I had to break it up."

Anya gnawed the inside of her cheek to restrain her tongue.

"I'll bet one of my bullets got him at the warehouse," he hissed.

Her fingers tightened on the trigger. "I could kill you right now without hesitation."

Sun used his index fingernail to clean under his thumbnail." I don't think you've ever killed anyone in your life."

"There's always a first time for everything. A bullet here, a bullet there, doesn't mean you die."

Sun's eyes shifted to his cane.

"Give me a reason." She leaned forward.

"I want to show you something." He reached into his inside jacket pocket.

"Easy does it," she said.

"Maybe we can strike a deal." Sun withdrew a small black velvet bag. "A woman gave me a gift after I saved her husband trapped under fallen debris." He shook the bag over a small table below the window in between the chair and bench seat. A metal object fell out and rolled around before it settled.

Anya blinked, then her jaw dropped. She strained to comprehend what lay in front of her. She collapsed in her seat. "God," passed her lips as she clutched at her blouse. Bile burned in her esophagus and she tightened her throat to keep it down. An Asscher cut red diamond with blue sapphires lay on the tabletop. Her ring.

She screamed out, "You bloody bastard." She stood, put the barrel to Sun's skull, and cocked the hammer.

Sun stared at her with a blank expression. "What?"

Her eyes fixed tight to the jewel. "Mamma

would never have offered my ring to the likes of you."

"Your mother?" Sun guffawed. "You're Colonel Pavlovitch's daughter?" Sun clapped his hands and threw his head back. "How poetic."

Anya said, "How did you get this?"

"I'll tell you, if you lower your weapon."

She swallowed her rage, retracted the hammer, and sat.

Sun rested his elbows on his knees, his face close to hers. His eyes cast a repulsive glee in anticipation of relaying his tale.

"A recruitment group of Lenin's Reds came to our village. They were looking for men to help incite civil disobedience in the Hunan and Jiangxi provinces. They trained me to kill, although it was more of a slaughter. No thrill in mowing down people. The scar you see," he ran his finger across the old wound, "it's from that time. I've since learned to become an expert at," he paused. "Elimination." He flaunted a wide grin.

"If you are trying to mess with my mind, it's not working," she said.

He shrugged and leaned back. "Lenin recruited my skills for a special assignment. Once the White Army fell, my assignment was to hunt down and eradicate all those who might return to usurp his control.

"Cut off the head of the snake and the body will die." Sun held a stony expression. "I found Admiral Kolchak and Colonel Pavlovitch in Irkutsk. Kolchak, fortunately, met his fate, but your father evaded my trap."

Anya conjured images of her father struggling to escape this monstrous man.

"In Vladivostok, the Colonel had jumped aboard a steamer. I caught up with him again months later in Shanghai. It wasn't hard to find a Russian, in a city filled with Chinese.

She flashed on Paval's letter. Sun had been the man who threatened him into revealing her father's location.

"I tracked him for days waiting for the right opportunity. Then one night, a night of miracles." Sun lifted his head has if to pray. "The gods delivered to me an earthquake. What better way for an assassin to cover his tracks than a street full of mayhem.

"Your mother became frantic when I emerged from the shadows. She cried and pleaded and begged for my help." Sun imitated a woman's voice. "Help me. My husband is injured."

Anya dug her nails into her leg.

"He laid trapped, under building rubble, like an animal in a snare." Sun laced his fingers behind his head. "If it's any consolation, your father would have died from his injuries. I put him out of his misery."

Anya sat still, as though in a trance, while words continued to pour from Sun's lips.

"I had no quarrel with your mother, just bad luck she happened to accompany your father. And as for the ring, why leave it for someone else to pinch?"

Anya fought back the tears and wiped her nose with the back of her hand. She rose from her seat then pointed the pistol at Sun's groin. "I'm going to shoot you in places that will cause excruciating pain but allow you to live."

An unexpected moan from Mac caused her to turn.

Sun took the opportunity to grab his cane and swing it at Anya's knuckles. She yelped, dropped the gun. It slid across the floor towards the door where Mac lay. He slapped her to the ground. She lay between the table and the chair.

Sun pulled the silver cap off the top of the cane, exposing a six-inch steel knife and came at her. "This is the same knife that I used on your parents," he said.

Anya raised one arm to her face and with the other tried to reach for the Mauser on the chair.

A sudden muffled pop stopped Sun and he grabbed his side. He stared down at his blood-covered hand. Anya looked beyond Sun to see Mac on one elbow with a .38 in hand. Sun fell to his knees and released his grip on the cane.

"Making friends I see." Mac rose and offered her help up.

An outpouring of relief swept over her. "You've got to stop getting knocked out." She took a deep breath. "My nerves can't handle it."

He rubbed his head. "My skull can't take much more."

Sun's lip tightened with one corner curled up. Anya picked up the cane and made an effort to swing at him. Before she could make contact, Mac grabbed her arm and pulled her back "I need to question him, before you kill him."

"Better hurry. I don't know how much longer I can restrain myself." She tapped the cane against her palm.

A voice from the other side of the washroom hollered, "What happened?"

"Shut up, or we'll shoot you too," Anya yelled.

"Who's that?" Mac said. Anya did not have time to answer him before they heard footsteps from outside the cabin. She watched Mac jump into the hallway, leaving her to guard Sun.

She poked her head out the door to see a man barrel down the corridor then halt in his tracks when he saw Mac's gun. From his uniform, she deduced he must be the engineer.

"What's he saying?" Mac held his arms straight with the gun in both hands.

"He's so excited I can't make it out. Something about the Japanese," Anya replied.

"Tell him to pull out of the station. Say his life depends upon it."

Anya relayed Mac's instructions. The engineer stood motionless. Mac moved in and forced the muzzle into the man's mouth. "Tell him once more."

Before Anya had time to reiterate, the engineer raised his hands, then turned on his heels.

"Stay with Sun. I'm going forward. Will you be all right?" Mac said.

Anya slid the ring on her finger, admired it for a moment. She turned to Sun and stuck the knife into his thigh as if to test a well-done pot roast. He let out a loud moan.

"We'll be just fine."

THIRTY-FIVE

ANYA HELD ON to the knife in one hand and the Mauser in the other. Sun sat on the floor with his head back against the bench seat. Blood formed a pool at his side where Mac shot him and trickled down from his thigh where Anya had stabbed him. His breath was shallow with only the whites of his eyes visible.

Her cold stare rendered little sympathy for his pain. She imagined the pleasure she would receive from plunging his own dagger into his beating heart.

The train lurched forward and moved slowly down the tracks. Mac came in from the engine room.

"Where are we headed?" Anya said.

Mac peered at Sun. "West."

"Dai Li?" Anya turned her lip up.

Mac nodded.

Sun tried to pull himself up but Mac stepped on him. Sun grimaced.

A loud thump from the rear of the train froze Anya and Mac. They fixed their eyes on each other. Anya stuck her head out the window. "Jesus." She felt the blood drain from her face. "Japanese soldiers."

Mac released his hold on Sun. "Watch him, I'll be right back."

Mac sprinted through the dining car with the .38. He saw a soldier making his way onto the back rail of the last car while others ran to catch up. Mac ran back to the sleeper car and climbed down into a small open space between the two cars and proceeded to uncouple it.

The smell of hot metal filled his nose when he unhinged and detached the vacuum pipe. He swiveled the coupling rod several times to loosen the large chain. Before he had a chance to unhook the chain, a bullet whizzed near his head. Mac jumped to his feet and returned fire at a soldier who ran alongside the train. His shot caught the man in the chest but others were close behind.

Mac fell on his belly with a groan. His ribs still ached and he winced while he resumed uncoupling the car. He only needed to pull the chain over the hook and they would be free of it. Less weight would allow them to travel at a faster speed. But there was no slack in the chain. He had to wait for the bar to relax before he could unhook the cars. Meanwhile, he heard additional soldiers climbing aboard.

Mac checked the gun. There were three bullets in the chamber. He wished he had taken the Mauser instead. It had more rounds.

The train jerked then turned a sharp corner. He only had seconds to unhook the two cars. Without thought, he placed the gun on the landing. The engine lurched forward causing the two cars to slam together. This gave Mac the opportunity to flip the hook off; simultaneously the gun slid off the landing and fell on the other car's coupler. Mac stretched out his arm. It was less than an inch away. His fingertips touched the gun but he failed to grasp it as the train gained speed.

No longer protected by the last car, Mac dashed inside as several soldiers tried to outrun the train.

"I HEARD SHOOTING." Anya sat on the bench seat with Sun at her feet. "What's going on?"

"We have a problem." Mac glanced down at

Sun. "Is he dead?"

"Not sure," she said.

"We need to put distance between ourselves and this train."

"Why?"

"I just killed a couple of soldiers."

"Great. I hope you know you've just poked a stick into a beehive."

"Hence, the reason to exit. There will be a mass of patrols along these tracks. And we've got to get off before we pick up real speed."

"What about him?" Anya poked Sun with the knife. Sun remained motionless.

Mac bent down and placed his fingertips on Sun's neck. "I'm not feeling a pulse. In any case he'll be dead in under an hour with the amount of blood he has lost."

Anya placed the tip of the blade at Sun's chest and thought about the lives this maniacal, evil, twisted man had altered. Tears welled up and her hand trembled. Images of Paval and his family arose then the faces of her mother and father surfaced.

"Anya," Mac yelled. "We have to leave now."

The knife slid from her fingertips.

ANYA AND MAC positioned themselves in the

opening between the car and the engine. The smell of burning coal filled the air. The engineer with his eyes on the two of them continued to stoke the engine furnace.

Anya stepped down onto the metal step. "Remember to tuck and roll onto your shoulder," Mac said.

Anya jumped into the darkness. Clouds masked the moonlight. She landed in tall grass that whipped across her face. It held the smell of fresh cut lemons. She felt relieved she had managed to roll and not dislocate her shoulder or wrench an ankle. In the distance, Mac let out a muffled moan.

Anya whispered. "Where are you?"

"Follow my voice," Mac said. "Keep moving forward, I can almost see you."

She remained crouched as she neared him and halted when his fingers touched her arm. "Is it your ribs?"

"They're a little sore but I can walk."

"Good, the stone bridge near the Chapei District is a short distance from here."

"What's there?" Mac said.

"Bia."

"The Communist?"

Darkness disguised her displeasure at his concern. "She's a friend. And in these uncertain times one friend can prove more invaluable than an entire army."

"You're right. What's the plan?" Mac said.

"When I contacted Bia the other day, she said they were heading up to the communist's stronghold in Yan'an. She said they'd be docked by the river if I wanted help to get out of Shanghai. She agreed to wait on the river at the stone bridge for two nights."

"Sounds like a solid plan."

"I do have a few good ideas."

They continued to wade through tall grass. The clouds dissipated and lent light from the full moon.

"No ring around the moon," he said.

"Good fortune," she said.

"We could use some."

"That we could." When they arrived at a dirt road, Anya turned left.

"How do you know which direction to take?" Mac said.

"I can tell by the position of the moon in the sky."

They had been walking for quite a while before Mac piped up. "You know, the moon can't give you directions."

Anya chuckled. "I know but it seemed the only way to get you to move and avoid an argument."

Mac laughed.

"Why did you agree to follow?" Anya said.

"You guessed right."

"What do you mean?"

"Stop a moment." Mac stood behind Anya then took her arm and lifted it to the skies. He led her arm from a starting point down then straight across then up then over. "Do you see those stars?" Anya nodded.

"Here in the northern hemisphere, it's known by a number of names the Big Dipper, Ursa Major, The Bear, Saucepan. See the star at the end of the bowl?"

"Yes."

"That's Dubhe. If you follow it up, you will find Polaris or the North Star. See how it sparkles greater than the other stars. Once you have the North Star in your sites, you know all other directions."

"Did you learn that in the Navy?"

"Yeah." Mac smiled and shuffled his feet in the dirt. "They say thousands of years from now the Dipper will reform and we won't recognize it. Kinda messes with your mind, if you think about it."

Anya's muscles became rigid at the sounds of a distant rumble. They both locked eyes. "Whatever it is, it's big," Mac said. "Quick, hide in the ditch face down. Make sure your hands are covered too."

Anya followed Mac's instructions. The sound of the convoy grew more intense, almost deafening. She was unsure if it was fear or the ground's vibration that caused her body to tremble. Several vehicles passed by then one stopped. They heard a door squeak open. Footsteps neared. Above her, she heard a Japanese soldier yell back "I'm hurrying." Anya's heart raced so hard her fingertips pulsated. She heard the tinkle sound then the smell of urine next to her head. The man zipped himself up, ran back to his vehicle and sped off.

It was several moments before she felt safe enough to exhale. But she still kept still. After several minutes Mac said, "I think we're in the clear. Are you okay?"

"It was almost comical had I not been so terrified."

"I'm sure they are on their way to catch that train," Mac said.

"Hopefully they won't bother checking the river."

"Don't count on it," he said.

They continued down the dirt road for several miles with caution. Both remained quiet in their own thoughts.

Noises in the distance once again caused them to stop. "Listen," Anya said. "We must be near the river. Voices are louder and more distinct when carried over water." She sensed her cheeks burn from embarrassment. "You probably already knew that?"

Mac gave her a boyish grin.

They crept towards the clatter that lay beyond a clump of trees that hugged the riverbank. Numerous sampans moored along the bank held glowing lights that flickered through their cloth canopies. Yards down the river a stone arched bridge rose to meet the moonlight.

Anya cupped her hands closed and blew between her thumbs causing a sharp whistle. She blew again, this time fluttered her fingers giving off a melodic sound similar to a bird. They waited in the darkness.

"Maybe we should get closer to the bridge," Mac said.

"No, if she's around she'll have heard it. I'll try once more." Anya wiped the sweat from her hands on her trouser leg. Before she had the chance to signal again, a chirp like a beetle rang out.

"Anya?" A voice called out from the dark.

"Bia. It's us," Anya replied.

"We're over here." Bia waved them over.

Anya and Mac climbed aboard the makeshift boat with its hodgepodge of different types of wood. It was no longer than fifteen feet and four feet wide. A tall Chinese man stood at the bow. Anya recognized Bia's husband and acknowledged him with a nod.

Anya knew from the expression on Bia's face that Mac was a surprise. She had expected Guy. "Long story, I'll tell you later," she said.

"We were informed about a shooting at the North Station," Bia said. "They have patrol boats, road blocks, and attack dogs hunting everywhere."

"Yeah, we dodged a troop a ways back," Mac said.

"You'll need to hide until we are outside of Shanghai," Bia said.

Bia pulled up several floor planks exposing a hollowed out space in the hull. Mac raised an eyebrow at Anya. She ignored his innuendo and climbed down into the hole. The odor of damp rotting wood filled her nostrils as she nestled into the tight quarters.

Bia tossed in a couple blankets. "We plan to travel slowly up the river to avoid catching anyone's attention. Dawn will break in a few hours. With any luck we should be far away from here when it does." Bia rearranged the boards back in place.

A glimmer of light from the lantern shone between the cracks, then it went pitch dark. They lay on their backs side by side. The tight fit gave little mobility. Anya felt the sampan move and a whooshing sound as it glided across the water.

"Now we know how they arm themselves," Mac said.

"Shush, they'll hear you."

"I, I want to tell you something . . . without you getting upset."

She stiffened. "Oookay."

"Back at the warehouse," he said. "I want to . . . I just don't want this day to finish without saying thank you."

"Don't get maudlin on me," she said. "Seems out of character."

"Tell me," Mac said, "Why'd you drop the knife instead of plunging it into Sun's eye socket."

Anya rubbed her ring band with her thumb. The cool metal felt good against her skin. "I reflected on the young girl my parents raised and the promise of the woman they wished me to become. At that moment, I felt my parents with me." She cleared her throat. "I refused to kill him in an act of anger because then, he would be with me always."

"To not lose yourself in someone else's evil takes courage," Mac said. "I admire your valor."

"Sun considered himself a soldier and he died without honor. That was the greatest punishment I could bestow."

"That's my girl." Mac chuckled.

"What about you? You didn't find Li. What will you do now?"

"We're not out of China yet and heading towards his last known location."

"Don't be a hero Mac. Don't forget you have a wife and child."

"Duty comes before family."

DAWN'S LIGHT SEEPED through the spaces between the boards. Anya opened her eyes. Confusion washed over her and her mind raced then she remembered they were hiding in a sampan. Next to her, Mac snored.

"Anya," Bia called out.

"Yes."

"Wake your friend. There are soldiers ahead. You both need to be silent or we will all be shot."

Anya nudged Mac with her elbow. He awoke with a snort. "Yeah, I'm up."

"Be quiet," Anya snapped, "soldiers are approaching." Instinctively, she turned the ring so the stone resided on the inside of her hand.

The patrol engine throttled down and came alongside. Its wake rocked the sampan, causing them to knock into each other. Barking orders from a soldier resonated. Anya felt her fears start to bubble up.

Mac slid his hand onto hers and held it tight. Anya felt his perspiration. His fear somehow reassured her. She closed her eyes and slowed her breathing.

The sampan took a dramatic tilt to one side, then heavy footsteps reverberated on the deck. Dark shadows flashed by from above and dirt fell in between the gaps. She blinked from the grit that washed around. She held her breath and pinched her nose to squelch a sneeze.

Metal and wood crashed to the floor. Anya heard Bia cry out and became rigid. She had a strong urge to kick open the floorboards, jump out of her hole, and rescue her friend. Mac squeezed her hand as though he knew what she contemplated. There was a tussle of two people, several smacks, and then something heavy fell to the deck. Tears trickled down the sides of Anya's cheeks. Voices grew louder. Anya could not distinguish one from the other nor understand what they were saying.

Their eyes followed the footsteps as the soldier walked from one end to the other, then they stopped directly over their heads. Anya and Mac held their breaths. They heard the sound of some-one rummaging through something, then Bia's tone pleaded for him to take something and leave them in peace.

The footsteps inched towards Bia's voice then the sampan tipped to one side again and the patrol boat roared off.

Bia knocked on the plank. "They've gone. We will head up river a few miles before it's safe for you to come out."

"Bia, are you hurt?" Anya said.

"We're fine. They were looking for anything of value to steal. The slimy buggers," Bia said. "I gave him a piece of jade carved in the shape of a scarab."

298 • P. C. Chinick

"Was it of great value?" Anya said.

"No, it's a trinket the locals make to export to Westerners. We keep them around for just that reason."

Anya exhaled, "I'm glad everyone is all right."

Hours later, Anya and Mac unfolded themselves from their hiding spot. Anya squinted from the bright daylight then rubbed her eyes. On deck, they stretched their backs and took in the fresh air. The sun, now high in the sky, caressed their bodies.

Anya glanced at the back of the boat where Bia's husband propelled the sampan with a long sculling oar. His left eye appeared red and swollen. She knew he had been in the struggle.

"I'm sorry for getting you involved, Bia."

"He's fine," Bia said. "It's not the first time we've encountered these patrol boats. Take a seat forward. We have a long journey ahead of us. I'll prepare something to eat."

Mac collapsed on the wooden bench and massaged his ribs.

"You look feverish." Anya plopped next to him. "We'll have to find someone to look at that."

"It's just a wicked bruise. I'll be okay."

Anya admired her ring and polished the diamond

with her finger.

"Your face has taken on a different look. A peaceful quality," Mac said.

"I realize a part of me had been missing all these years. As if I'd lost an arm or a leg and now it's been sewed back on. I'm whole again. I promised my parents long ago that I would never lose this ring or myself. I never will."

Mac pointed to the necklace around her neck "What about that? Did you give yourself the same pledge?"

"You think this is a gift from Guy?" she said.

Mac lowered his head and shrugged.

She held the pendant in her hand. "The rightful owner of this is Edmund Atwater."

"I see." Mac raised his head then rubbed his chin. "Interesting. You just might make a spy yet."

Anya rolled her eyes. "All I want to think about right now is going home." She tried to imagine where home might be. San Francisco held too many memories and Shanghai was an impossibility.

The river narrowed as they traveled inland. Lush greenery hung along the riverbank and the sun shimmered off the river's smooth surface. Anya hung her arm over the edge and let the water flow between her fingers. She felt an inner peace and was thankful she had made the trek.

She leaned back, closed her eyes, and let the sun

warm her. A strange image entered her thoughts. It appeared unknown to her yet familiar. She focused to see an outline of a face. The eyes were closed. Then a nose, a mouth came into focus. She struggled to recognize the figure. Who is it? she thought.

A black lifeless shark-eyed stare threw her back. She knew in an instant, it was Sun Temujin. He whispered, "I'll find you, Anya."

ASSCHER DIAMOND COMPANY

The Asscher Diamond Company was founded in 1854 by the Asscher family of Amsterdam. Developed in 1902, the deeply square cut corners gives the Asscher cut an almost octagonal outline. It features a small table, high crown, broad step facets, deep pavilion and square culet. It was an extreme departure from the brilliant cuts that dominated the 1800s and was a forerunner of the standard emerald cut.

When the Nazis entered Amsterdam during WWII they seized all of Asscher's diamonds and interned the family in concentration camps. Only ten members survived internment. During that time the patent on the original Asscher cut expired, leaving the family to start again after the war ended.

In 1980, the once Asscher Diamond Company become known as the Royal Asscher Diamond Company. The Asscher family secured an international design patent to protect the Royal Asscher cut so it cannot be legally imitated; Royal Asscher is also trademarked and the company owns exclusive rights to the name.

ABOUT THE AUTHOR

P. C. Chinick, grew up in the Pacific Northwest and now resides in Northern California. She spent the majority of her professional career in information technology and earned an M.B.A. in international business from John F. Kennedy University. When the tech bubble burst she took up her one passion, writing. Ms. Chinick is the current President of California Writers Club Tri-Valley Branch.

You can read more about Anya Pavlovitch's story at www.redasscher.com/blog.

CPSIA information can be obtained at www.ICGtesting.com
Printed in the USA
BVOW08s0033100214

344357BV00001B/1/P

9 780991 197309